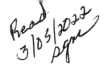

PRAISE FOR SPIN

"With fresh, fast-paced storytelling and a personable, self-deprecating protagonist, McKenzie whirls a perfectly indulgent tale."

—Publisher's Weekly

"McKenzie endows what could have been a formulaic, tired plot with finely drawn characters, broad humor, and a sweet and satisfying romance between equals. Her descriptions of rehab are as candid as they are sympathetic. She is a writer to watch."

—Booklist

"If *Bridget Jones's Diary* and *High Fidelity* had a literary baby, the result would be *Spin*. A funny heroine and plentiful music references make this book a stand out. McKenzie's tale of girls gone wild and gone to rehab is ripped straight from the latest tabloid headlines and will keep readers intrigued to the very last page."

—RT Magazine (Top Pick)

"McKenzie's deliciously tart sense of humor and her tough yet tender heroine are as refreshing as a perfectly mixed mimosa."

—Chicago Tribune

"Kate Sandford is someone you know: she's snarky and a little bit fragile, and when she has the chance to make up for blowing the opportunity of a lifetime, you can't help but root for her even when she's not rooting for herself. Catherine McKenzie has written a winning first novel—*Spin* is funny, touching, and impossible to put down."

—Shawn Klomparens, author of Jessica Z. and Two Years, No Rain

"Catherine McKenzie puts a comedic spin on a heavy reality in her engaging novel, *Spin*. In the hands of vibrant and endearing Kate, rock bottom has never felt so relatable, or brought such a sense of adventure to readers. *Spin* touches on the indefatigable theme of redemption and gives a tale as old as time a fresh voice. An addicting page-turner, *Spin* is the perfect escape with a delicious side of eye-opening discovery."

—Examiner.com

"*Spin* is a compelling, fast-paced read."
—*The Globe and Mail* (Toronto)

"With McKenzie's engaging debut, you'll be up late rooting for the loveable and broken Kate Sandford as she stumbles her way towards sobriety by way of a bit of tabloid journalism. *Spin* is honest, funny, and fresh."
—Julie Buxbaum, author of *The Opposite of Love* and *After You*

"In Kate Sandford, Catherine McKenzie has created a 21st-century Bridget Jones—dark and delicate, broken yet strong."
—Tish Cohen, author of *Inside Out Girl* and *Town House*

"Imagine if Bridget Jones fell into a million little pieces, flew over the cuckoo's nest, and befriended Lindsay Lohan along the way, and you are beginning to grasp the literary roller coaster ride that is Catherine McKenzie's *Spin*. Filled with brutal honesty and wry humor, *Spin* is a story for anyone who has every woken up hungover and thought, 'Do I have a problem? Yes—I need to find a greasy breakfast.' And by that I mean everyone I know."
—Leah McLaren, author of *The Continuity Girl*

"*Spin* is intelligent, poignant, and a bit of rollicking, good fun."
—Cathy Marie Buchanan, *New York Times* bestselling author of *The Painted Girls*

"*Spin* is a fresh, sassy, and compelling novel delivered with pitch-perfect humor. McKenzie's light touch with a serious topic will have readers cheering for Kate as she proves people *can* change."
—Holly Kennedy, author of *The Penny Tree*

"With *Spin*, Catherine McKenzie taps into both the ridiculous and sublime elements of the world her character inhabit, and, more importantly, points out how those are often exactly the same. A thoroughly engaging debut."
—David Sprague, Music Journalist, contributor to *Variety*, *Village Voice* and *Rolling Stone*

SPUN

Catherine McKenzie

MONTREAL

2014

For everyone who read Spin,
and asked for something more.

ISBN-13: 978-0-692-02516-1
ISBN-10: 0-692-02516-2

Chapter 1

Dirt and Dead Ends

This is how it starts.

It's the end of a very long day, one of those craptastic ones where you wish you could just fast-forward past the bad parts, like your life's something you've DVRd, and the bad parts are the commercials. Only it's late-night TV, wall-to-wall commercials, and that ShamWow!® guy has bought all the airtime.

The day begins at 5 a.m. I'm up this early because I'm shooting a commercial for my new perfume, Fabulous by Amber Sheppard.

Seriously. That's what they made me call it.

Fabulous, I ask you?

Does anyone look at my life these days and think, *Fabulous?*

So it's 5 a.m., and I couldn't sleep last night because I can never sleep when I have to get up at 5 a.m., and the driver waiting for me outside my building is not the usual nice, reliable Dave who doesn't think I'm ridiculous for needing a driver, like this guy seems to.

As if I need the judgment.

As if I haven't been judged enough.

But this guy is all judgment, from the up-and-down sweep he does of me—still in my pajamas, hair unbrushed, sneakers, no makeup—to the way he slams the door after I climb in, hesitating long enough to let me know he thinks I should've closed it myself.

This guy is clearly in the wrong profession, but I get a sense of where his attitude might be coming from when he moves a magazine off his seat in a way that's sure to catch my attention.

It's the new *People*, me on the cover. I seem to be driving drunk, not because I was, but because they caught me at a bad moment, at an intersection, when I closed my eyes for a second. But my hair's a mess, my mascara's running, and the way they framed the shot, I seem to be passed out. And the fact that I haven't had a drink in two years and twenty-seven days, well, no one's going to believe that, right? Not even if I show them the chips I have to prove it.

Not when they have the photo evidence to the contrary.

I know well enough by now not to act guilty simply because other people think I should, so I give the driver a defiant look in the rear-view, lay my head back, and close my eyes.

Go ahead. Take a picture. Tell the world you drove a drunk and disheveled Amber Sheppard to some gig at sunrise.

I don't care.

Just let me sleep until I get there.

The commercial's being filmed about an hour outside the city in one of those steam-and-pipe factories that always get used for foot-chase scenes in the movies. In fact, this is what the script for the Fabulous by Amber Sheppard ad spot calls for; someone chasing a desperate me through a factory.

"So they can catch me and smell my perfume?" I asked at the creative meeting.

"No," said the director after a moment of shocked silence—how dare I question his vision? "It's an ironic metaphor. Because you're hunted, you're prey, but you're still—"

"Fabulous. Right. I get it."

I'm pretty sure the whole thing is neither ironic nor a metaphor, but nobody ever appreciates it when I point out that sort of thing. So I keep quiet even though I think it's a dumb idea, overdone and obvious. But I don't have much say in these things anymore, as my agent, Bernard, is fond of reminding me. I'm lucky they wanted to take a chance on me. Lucky I can still find work, even if it's in a crappy, bad-ironic-metaphor-that's-neither-of-those-things commercial for a smells-like-a-mix-of-dandelions-and-maple-sugar perfume.

Lucky.

I can feel the *buzz, buzz* of my phone through the fabric of the bag sitting next to me, little electric shocks that have me Pavlovian-reaching for it, though I know I shouldn't. Only two people would be texting me at this hour: Bernard to ask me why I'm [insert expletive of your choice] not on set yet, and a man whose texts I shouldn't return.

I reach inside and wrap my hand around the phone anyway,

breathing in and out slowly, trying to fight the urge to check it. It double buzzes again, and with my heart pounding, I pull it out and sneak a peek at the preview bar floating on the screen.

It's Bernard.

Where the fuck ru? his text reads when I open it.

Some people are so predictable.

★

Bernard is waiting for me at the factory's spray-painted industrial door. He's illuminated by a set of bright arc lights. There's a beehive of people behind him, bustling about with camera equipment and set dressings.

Keep Out, someone's scrawled on the door in bright yellow spray paint, and I want to obey.

"Wild fucking night?" Bernard asks, his voice a rasp.

Fifty, short, and foul-mouthed, Bernard's the best in the business and the only reason I still have any work. He's been my agent since I was seventeen. I know why he took me on then—my career was all shiny and bright, and I hadn't yet fulfilled the predictions that I'd end up as an *E! True Hollywood Story* in the "Child Stars Gone Wrong" week. Why he's still around after I've fulfilled that promise (and more) is something I'm too nervous to ask him. If I start questioning his presence, he might wise up and leave.

"Couldn't sleep," I say.

"We're wasting dollars."

"I'm five minutes late."

He shakes his head. His skull shines through his shortly shaved hair. "How many times do I have to tell you? You gotta be fucking early so no one says you're late."

"Okay, Bernard."

My phone buzzes again. My fingers itch to reach for it.

"Hair and Makeup is waiting for you."

I meet his grey eyes. "I'm on it."

"You've got to murder this today."

"I'll die for it."

"That's my girl."

✪

The next twelve hours are an assembly line of pain.

Hair made "fabulous," and then disheveled. Ditto makeup. A diaphanous gown is draped and cut so they'll probably have to CGI over parts of me to be able to run the ad on TV. There's steam and smoke, and the Ironic Metaphor Director screaming, "You're not scared enough! Stop looking like you know you're going to *survive*. Put your life on the *line*."

As per the conditions of my insurance bond, I am never left alone, not even to go to the bathroom. Especially not then. If I so much as ask for a tissue, I can feel a room full of eyes staring at my nose, searching for traces of powder, for evidence of failure, weakness.

All of which makes me want to fail, to be weak.

My phone keeps buzzing. Every hour, three minutes past the hour, a secret code, like ringing two times before you hang up.

I resist, I resist, I resist.

We wrap around six p.m. I'm shivering and exhausted and beyond knowing if I've done enough, but after Bernard and the director have a quick consultation, they declare themselves satisfied and I'm released.

Now I'm allowed to be alone. I stand under the fizzing spray of the dirty, makeshift shower they set up in a corner of the bathroom behind a plastic curtain that affords no privacy. The water's lukewarm and it doesn't help dispel the deep chill that's taken root in my bones. Or the itch, the bloody itch, to check my phone and confirm what I already know.

I turn off the water and wrap myself in a fluffy, white bathrobe, the only fabulous thing I've seen all day. The buzz of my phone shivers through the floor and my will dissolves.

There are twelve unread texts from his number today. Two months full of them behind that, less regular but persistent. We haven't spoken for six months. I haven't returned any of his texts.

But today's texts all say the same thing:

Babe, renkonti min . . .

Babe, renkonti min . . .

Our secret, private language adopted years ago as a joke. As a code it was easy to break, but that was never the point of it.

What's important are the words. Because we agreed long ago to only use them when we mean them.

Meet me, baby . . .

Meet me, baby . . .

The last text has a location and a time: an airport forty-five minutes away, where I need to be an hour from now. For what, the text doesn't say.

But he used our magic words, and so I change quickly back into my pajamas—the only clothes I have—and slip outside before anyone can stop me, directing the Judgmental Driver to take me where I shouldn't go.

✪

The number of paparazzi at the airport almost makes me ask him to turn around and leave.

Almost.

Despite his obvious reluctance, the Judgmental Driver pushes the town car through the crowd slowly, edging the paparazzi out of the way. The tinted windows keep me anonymous, for now. But like hunters on the prowl for big game, they can sense their prey. They've been waiting for hours, and they want what they've come for.

They're about to get more than that.

A security guard steps out to stop us at the gate to the private airstrip. The Judgmental Driver lowers the window and tells him my name. The guard's eyes go round. He knocks on my window anyway, wanting proof. I lower it enough so he can see me. My black hair, my trademark widow's peak, my sure-to-be-bloodshot green eyes. I couldn't look more the part I'm about to play if I tried, and he nods us through quickly.

Not quickly enough, though, as one eagle-eyed pap screams my name, half in shock, half in victory. Arms go up, bulbs flash, shutters snap, and only the security guard's hand on the holster of his Taser keeps the crowd from leaping on the car like it's a lone deer that's wandered away from the herd.

My hands are shaking and my heart feels like it's going to explode. My mouth fills with the taste of formaldehyde and smoke and pain.

But I don't tell the driver to turn around.

I don't say anything.

He stops the car as close to the private plane's stairs as he can. I open the door before the engine cuts and bolt up them. A flight attendant in a 1950s uniform grabs my arm on the top step, pulling me through and shutting the cabin door behind me.

I catch my breath, taking in my surroundings. The inside of the plane looks like it's been dressed for a bad rap video. Two massive bodyguards in black T-shirts are spilling out of their seats, sweeping the room with menacing gazes, as if someone might be thinking of making an attempt on someone's life. Four or five girls wearing skimpy skirts, plunging necklines, and sporting orangey tans are draped over various members of his entourage. Bottles of Crystal are strewn across almost every surface. A bass line booms from the speakers. There's even a bowl full of a powdery substance sitting on a glass coffee table.

A black-haired head is hunched over the table, just finishing a line. He straightens up, holding his nose in a practiced pinch. He shakes his shoulders and looks me in the eye.

Connor Parks is five feet away from me.

And I'm shaking.

He smiles that slowly drawn smile of his and beckons me with a flick of his hand. I shake my head slightly. Looking like it's no big deal, as if we can't hear the shouts of the crowd outside, that their flashes aren't stuttering through the windows, as if everyone in the room hasn't stopped to watch, Connor rises, crosses the room, and stands in front of me. Waves of love, longing, sadness, and hurt crash over me. I'm re-feeling every moment we had together over the last ten years, from that first rush of crush to the final, final separation we had six months ago when I moved all of my stuff out of his house.

I reach out to steady myself, my hand finding his warm forearm.

"You're here," he says.

"I'm here."

"I knew you'd come."

"Oh?"

Now I am acting to save my life.

"Temptation, baby. Never your strong suit."

He takes a step towards me. He smells like chemicals and Crystal

SPUN 7

and the worst idea I've had in a long time.

"Connor—"

The plane's engines start and drown out my words.

"We've begun taxiing to our runway." The captain's voice replaces the thumping bass. "Please sit down, put on your seatbelts, and turn off all electronic devices."

Two of the girls start to giggle. One of them is holding her phone awkwardly. I'm pretty sure she's recording The Reunion of the Decade, or whatever this disaster's going to get called in the Twitterverse as soon as she uploads it.

"We should sit," I say.

He shrugs. "Come on back."

He turns without waiting for me and I know where he's headed—the luxury suite he had installed at the back of the plane when he bought it with his *Young James Bond* money.

The flight attendant starts to push people gently into their seats. The skimpy girls laugh as they tighten their seatbelts.

And me?

I drop my bag to the floor and I follow him.

Like I always do.

Like I've been doing my whole life.

The plane lurches and bumps over the tarmac away from the popping flashbulbs. I walk unsteadily down the aisle, my eyes fixed on the back of Connor's neck.

"Please take your seats," the captain says again.

The engine's whine starts to hurt my ears, like a dog whistle.

Connor opens the door to his suite and waggles his fingers at me behind his back. He thinks he's being cute, his little victory symbol, his professed certainty that I'd come, that I'm still at his beck and text.

Well, fuck that shit.

"No, no, no," I say, to myself, to him, to our audience. "I can't."

His shoulders tense, but before he can say anything, I turn on my heel and stumble away. I feel woozy and exhausted, like a riptide has me in its grip and I've been fighting it for hours, but I keep kicking.

I have to.

Though it must be against regulations, the door to the cockpit is half open. I lean against it in relief and collapse into the tiny room.

"What the hell?" the co-pilot says, swiveling in his seat.

"Let me off."

The pilot glances at me over his shoulder. "No can do. We've been cleared for takeoff."

"I mean it. Please. Let me off."

"You can get off when we stop to refuel in Miami."

"Wait. What? Where are we going?"

"The Bahamas."

"I can't."

"Just take your seat, all right?"

"No." My brain's whirring. "I . . . I don't have my passport. You have to let me off."

He sighs. "Christ."

"And," I continue, feeling desperate, pushing my luck, "if you don't, I'll tell customs about that little party that's going on back there."

His eyes narrow. "Get her the hell off my plane."

The co-pilot unbuckles himself and grabs me by the arm. The plane shudders to a stop as he releases the airlock. The stairs spill out into the night.

"Don't dally," he says, his voice gruff. "Move away from the plane quickly. The jets are on."

"Thank you."

I grab my bag and I'm down the stairs before they're fully deployed. I jump from the last step. The soles of my shoes slap against the concrete. I run towards the grass strip that divides this runway from the next. I trip over a light encased in the edge of the concrete and land on my hands and knees. The grass is wet with evening dew.

"Amber!"

I turn to face him. Connor's standing in the airplane's doorway looking, for once in his life, shocked. The co-pilot's trying to pull him away from the door as the stairs slowly rise.

"Amber!" he screams again, but I don't move. It takes everything I've got, but I hold fast to the damp grass, breathing in the cold night.

The door seals his last cry and the engines rev. The plane is moving, faster, *faster*, tipping up and into the sky, and I'm free.

Alone in the dark in the middle of an airfield.

But free.

✪

I get to my condo two hours later. It took me an hour of wrong turns to make it to the parking lot next to the hanger. The paparazzi I was half counting on to drive me home were long gone by then, off to sell their photos. But Connor's vintage BMW was still there, a spare key attached by a magnet under the front left wheel, as I knew it would be because he's always losing his keys.

When I get close to my building I realize I don't have my garage pass and I can't remember the combination, so I circle a couple of blocks till I find street parking.

One of Connor's baseball hats is sitting on the passenger seat. I tuck my hair up into it, just in case someone's staking out the back entrance to my building. All I need is a picture of me, in grass- and sweat-stained pajamas, stumbling into my building in what will look like the dead of night, though it's only a little after ten.

I let myself into my place, feeling as if I could sleep for a week. My clothes fall like breadcrumbs marking a path to my bedroom. Naked, I crawl under the covers as a terrible case of the shakes clutches me.

I pull the duvet over my head, sobbing into the soft blackness until my body gives out.

And when I wake up, Connor is dead.

Chapter 2

Any Way You Shake It

Let me, as they say, set the scene.

I am fifteen years old. I'm the lead character on a television show called *The Girl Next Door*, a weekly laugh-track sitcom with more tracks than laughs. *Ba dum dum.* The show is, against all reason, a hit. I begin to be referred to as "TGND" in the press and, sometimes, in real life. Not that I'm complaining—I'm, as they say, #justsaying.

It's our second season, and as our popularity has increased, the quality of the actors they start hiring to play my love interests goes up. Playing The Girl Next Door's Guy of the Week has become a nice way for a boy to get his start in the business, though it's never a long-term gig.

TGND is a bit of a heartbreaker.

Fifteen-year-old me is in a moony mood. I have my head in the clouds. In the down moments on set, in between shots, I'm less focused. I'm daydreamy.

Maybe it's because my parents have been talking about getting divorced—again—and I've decided to believe in love rather than its end. Or maybe there isn't any explanation other than the fact that I'm fifteen.

Whatever the reason, I'm feeling like I should be falling in love. I'm ready to do some real heartbreaking. Plus I have a massive crush on the guy who plays my quirky but awesome dad, and even I know that's a bit creepy. More than one person has told me—kind of pointedly, but without any names being used—that there's no better way to cure a crush than to fall in love. (Beat.) "With someone your own age."

When I climb out from underneath the anvil of embarrassment, I make a deal with myself. I'm going to fall for someone more age-appropriate if it kills me.

So, I'm in the casting director's office because I know next week's script calls for the introduction of a new guy whose heart TGND will crush, and she'll have a stack of headshots to go through. I know this because, though I haven't seen the script yet, it's been three episodes since the last guy hit the road.

"No, no, too young, they can't be serious, already turned that guy down twice, hello. My, my, what do we have here?" Shawna, the casting director, says, holding one of the headshots by the corner like she didn't want to smudge it.

"Can I see?"

She makes as if to hug the photo to her chest, so now I really want to see it.

"Give it."

She hands it to me.

"Isn't he dreamy?" she asks. "I bet you totally fall for him."

"No one says 'dreamy' anymore, Shawna. Sheesh."

But he is.

So the scene is set, and Connor gets the part, and I'm primed for him. Even though he's eight years older than me—twenty-three playing sixteen—I fall for him hard. Maybe I would've fallen for anything that pretty put in my path at that moment. I tell myself that sometimes, to avoid thoughts like *destiny, cosmos, soulmate*. But that's what I felt from the first moment we met. My new heart, my new body, my young brain couldn't help thinking those things.

All the clichés applied. When we kissed, it felt like I'd never been kissed before. Happiness had a new high. And sadness had a different bottom too. In truth, I felt addicted. I needed more and more and more of him.

I couldn't get enough.

I could never get enough.

I thought it was like that for him too. Sometimes I knew it was, and sometimes the doubt crept in. In a weird way it didn't matter what he felt. Love like that is always selfish. I would've done anything for him, I did do anything he asked of me, but it wasn't for him. It was for me. To keep him with me. So I wouldn't lose him.

That's when the drugs came in. All fun, of course, at the beginning. That giggling first hit of hash at a party in the hills in a room full of beautiful people in a moment so scripted I sometimes can't remember if it was real or just some part I played.

But what came after that was certainly real. One party rolling into another. The first drink of the day taken to erase the scar left by the drinks of the night before. The first pill popped, just a pill, a bit of medicine, that looked like an Aspirin and didn't my head ache? Hadn't I had a long day working, working harder than any teenager should work?

Besides, Connor did it.

Connor did it.

✪

I know that something's wrong when I wake up in the klieg light blare of a thousand flashbulbs. I've never seen anything like it, not even the year I attended the Oscars as a nominee in a ballerina pink ball gown with a tutu skirt.

I was kind of hoping the Oscar-in-a-ballerina-pink-ball-gown juju would rub off on me.

It didn't.

But back to the lights.

Because the lights are so frickin' bright. It's still dark outside, yet my bedroom's lit up like a stage set.

There also seem to be helicopters circling my building, which is not that unusual, sorry to say, but which is also generally a precursor to bad news.

What the—oh, right. I went to see Connor last night. Not to mention the whole jumping out of a plane that was about to take off thing. Which one of those idiot girls clearly filmed on her phone and broadcast to the world before they took off.

Bernard must be apoplectic, and I'm so mad at myself right now I want to drink a million drinks until I erase myself.

That's the—you listening, Amber?—last, last, last time I ever do anything like that.

I am strong. I am stronger than that. I am stronger than him.

I've got to be.

I lie on my back and look at the beams illuminating my ceiling, cataloguing the night's stupidities. Despite their number, they still don't add up to helicopters.

Maybe Connor got busted when his plane landed? But they should still be in the air, right? I try to remember how long it takes to fly to Barbados. I mean the Bahamas. It was the Bahamas wasn't it?

I shake myself. The answers to my questions are just a click away. All I have to do is check the TV or my phone or Twitter; thousands of my 2.7 million followers are sure to have tweeted the worst of the links at me. It sounds so egotistical, but it's true. All I'd have to write is *Where's Connor?* and I'd have more information than necessary in a matter of seconds.

I just have to suck it up and face it.

I decide that the TV is probably my best option because, based on past experience, helicopters = TV coverage. And unlike my phone, at least it won't contain angry texts from Bernard, or my publicist, Olivia, or the sponsors of Fabulous by Amber Sheppard, etc.

It won't contain any messages from Connor, either.

I flick it on. It's tuned to CNN. It takes an instant for me to put together the images, the words crawling across the bottom of the screen.

When I can read them, this is what they say:

CONNOR PARKS' PLANE LOST DURING FLIGHT TO THE BAHAMAS . . . SEARCH AND RESCUE OPERATION UNDER WAY . . . NO SURVIVORS EXPECTED TO BE FOUND . . .

The answer to everything.

Just a click away.

✪

I don't leave my apartment for two days.

I don't leave my bed, really, other than to use the bathroom or stare into the fridge for half an hour at a time, knowing I should eat something, but finding nothing I can push past my closed-off throat. I'm a little over five feet tall, and I've never had much weight to spare. The yoga pants I've been wearing since I got the news are barely staying up.

They are no survivors.

They search and search, and eventually they start to find pieces of the plane. The wreckage is spread out over half a mile of crystal-blue ocean, pieces of metal reflecting up at the circling helicopters like a trail of shiny new pennies.

They send in the deep-sea divers. Despite the extent of the

wreckage, they find several bodies strapped into their seats, the impending crash apparently enough to finally get them to heed the captain's requests to buckle up.

Connor is one of them. One of the ones who was strapped in. I would have bet he wouldn't have been, no matter what, but I guess his innate fear of . . . well, everything really, finally cut through the coke and bravado.

Oh, Connor. Why did you wait till it was too late to start acting sensibly?

They actually show images from down there, if you can believe it. What am I saying? Of course you can believe it. Ghostly white faces, blurred by the water, shot on that camera James Cameron invented to film the wreckage of the *Titanic*. And me, big dummy, despite the warnings about the gruesome nature of what I'm about to see, I just sit there, watching it all, feeling myself shrink by the minute.

I keep watching as they hoist his body out of the ocean, a scene the networks intercut with images of Connor's fans standing in hands-clasped-over-their-mouths horror as they watch the news in the thousands of bars they've collected in to hold what feels like the world's biggest wake.

It's like one of those scenes in the old movies my film-buff dad made me watch when I was a kid, where you know an event is important because there are crowds standing outside electronic stores, eyes glued to the banks of television screens as they cast their bluish glow. And as I watch, I can't help but wonder if it's all fake—stock footage the networks pull out depending on the tragedy.

And then I think, *Oh my God.*

This isn't a movie, or a TV show, or some fake news scene.

This is my life.

The man I've loved forever is dead.

And it's another day before I speak to anyone.

Chapter 3

After Life

So, life's been pretty shit since I left rehab.

What? You didn't know about my stint(s) in rehab? Well, lucky for you, you can read all about it anytime you want, over and over—take last month's *Starlet* magazine for example:

ALL OUT OF COMEBACKS?
By Phyllis Hayes

I'm sitting in a café waiting for a star.

Two years ago today, the world watched as then It Girl, Amber Sheppard (*The Girl Next Door, Northanger Abbey, Chalet Party II*) escaped from rehab—her third stint that year—and led the police on a merry chase. After spending a few days out of sight, a video of her smoking crack emerged, which viralled its way to Internet most-watcheddom (over 10 million views in three days). A few days after that, her parents escorted her back to rehab, where she was joined shortly thereafter by her on-again, off-again boyfriend, Connor Parks (*The Young James Bond, Forgotten, Chalet Party III*).

When she completed her program thirty-eight days later, the world was ready to give her another chance.

She was our girl next door, after all.

All she had to do was ask . . .

That's the nicest piece anyone's written about me in years.

What was I saying? Oh, right, rehab.

That was fabulous. And it was life changing, okay; it really was. I mean, I did stop taking drugs and drinking and a bunch of other bad things I was doing to myself, and those were good changes, but, *but*, when I got out, I was also damaged goods.

Everyone deserves a second chance, right? That's what they tell you in rehab, NA, AA, all these anonymous people who, news flash, aren't really that anonymous, especially when they all know who you are.

That's what they say. That life's all about second chances. This is what makes you believe it's worth cleaning up your act, staying sober—that chance at a second chance. A different life than the hell you created for yourself.

But what I learned when I got out, what I guess I already knew on some level before that, and what was, if I'm being honest, one of things that kept me using, was that I'd used up all my chances. The second, the third, the fourth, the comeback after the fourth. The comeback after the comeback.

That was the cold reality waiting for me.

I'd burned all my matches, and then some.

So while I struggled to stay sober, people weren't rooting for me to succeed—they were hoping I'd fail. Preferably when someone could catch it on film.

Or at least it felt that way when the cameras were there to catch every little blunder and magnify it, manipulate it, or make it up if it didn't really happen.

She tripped on the sidewalk, in the middle of the day! Because she was drunk/high/crazy, of course. Of course.

She broke a cameraman's toe with her car! Because she was drunk/high/doesn't care about others, of course. Of course.

No matter about the broken heel that caused the fall, or the fact that there were so many cameras and hulking men surrounding my car, on my car, blocking my car, that I started having a panic attack and I warned them, like five times, that I was going to put the car in gear, that they'd better get out of the way.

But no matter, no matter.

My name is Amber Sheppard and I'm an alcoholic and a drug addict.

I did those things to myself when I had everything going for me, and I don't really expect people to feel sorry for me.

I really don't.

Only . . .

Life's been pretty shit since rehab.

✪

Despite Bernard doing everything he can to reach me except for knocking down my door with a battering ram, the first person I speak to, the first person I see, is my publicist and best friend, Olivia.

I met Olivia right after I turned seventeen. I was still caught up in the maelstrom that followed my legal emancipation from my parents (more about this later). My mom had always fielded press calls in the past—she liked the attention way more than I ever did—so I'd never understood how persistent the press could be. Or how they seem to have got my personal cell number, for that matter.

It was summer. I was at an outdoor table at the Gansevoort when a woman sitting at the next table asked, "You going to answer that?" after I'd angrily ignored three phone calls in a row.

I didn't know anyone at my table, though they all acted like they knew me. Connor was off God knows where doing God knows what. Well, okay, I have a pretty good idea, but it doesn't help to think about that. Especially not right now when I'm so beaten down by his death that all I can think about is using.

Anyway. Summer. The Gansevoort. Seventeen. One drink of many resting on the table in front of me.

"Unlikely," I said to the chatty stranger.

"Good."

This wasn't the answer I was expecting. I looked at her more closely. Twenty-five I guessed (though her IMDB page had her listed as twenty-one—"You have to think ahead," she'd tell me later), hair one shade lighter than her natural blonde, light green eyes, a few freckles across her nose. Cute made pretty by an expert makeup hand.

"You an actress?" I asked.

She smiled that bonded-teeth smile everyone around me seemed to have. "Trying. In the meantime, I do this."

"Sit at the Gansevoort?"

"Good one. You're funny, aren't you? They should play that up more on your show. Anyway, no. Or yes, in a manner of speaking. I do PR." She reached into her bag—one of those ones you had to be on a waiting list to get—and pulled out a card. "Olivia Proctor, Public Relations" it read in muted script. Somehow I'd expected something spangly, like her dress, or fake, like I was pretty sure her breasts were.

What a judgmental little punk I was.

"You could use me," she said.

"I . . . what?"

"Or someone like me. Someone better than me, probably. To handle your PR stuff."

My phone started to buzz on the table again. *Us Weekly* was calling. They weren't even trying to hide who they were anymore.

"I could keep that phone from ringing, for instance," she added.

"If you can keep my phone from ringing, you'll officially be my best friend for life."

She picked up my phone and dropped it into my glass.

"Does that position come with health insurance?" she asked, and I laughed.

✪

I don't want to see anyone, really, not even to prove to Bernard that I'm not about to fatally OD. But I have to admire Olivia for managing to get to my front door, given what's going on outside, and she has been with me through all the Connor stuff. The ups and downs and reunions and breakups and twists and turns and . . . you get the idea. Anyway, she's been there, you know, so I decide to let her be there for me today.

"Honey, you look terrible," she says when I've pulled her inside and taken the blanket off my head. I used it to cover up in case a photographer's made his way inside the building. "Have you been…"

She scans the room in a way I know means she's looking for evidence. An empty bottle. Dust on the table. Broken glass.

"Thanks a bunch."

"Oh, you know what I mean," she says, covering quickly. "What if someone besides me saw you?"

I slump onto my couch, pulling Connor's baseball cap down so it half covers my eyes. My yoga pants are starting to pill. Little black spots that have worn off them in the last few days are scattered across the ultra-white couch.

"Connor just died, Livvie. Who cares?"

Her face goes white and her lip quivers for a second, then she shakes it off. She puts her hands on her hips and cocks her head.

Her blonde ponytail swings back and forth, all glossy and perfect.

"No, no, no, no. Have I taught you nothing? Rule Number One of Being a Super Famous Person is—"

"—Always look your best."

"That's right. When Kim Kardashian made her first appearance after little North by Northwest was born, she looked like a million bucks, right?"

"It's North West."

"Huh?"

"The kid. Her name is North. West. Two words. How can you not know that?"

"Because, dear heart, as you well know, ever since Kanye started referring to himself as 'Yeezus,' I have refused to take in any knowledge associated with him or anyone related to him."

I suspect this stance actually has more to do with Kanye leaving me off a guest list or two in the last year, but I leave Olivia to her high moral ground.

"Okay, sure. But I don't see how that's relevant."

"What?"

"What Kim looked like. Her baby didn't die."

She snaps her French-manicured fingers loudly. "Life. Changing. Events. Focus."

I tuck my knees under my chin. "I still don't care."

She sits next to me and pulls my head to her shoulder. "I know, Amb, but that's what you pay me for. I care for you."

"I care for you too."

"A joke. Excellent. We'll have you in fake lashes and a . . ." She stops, considering. "What would be the appropriate outfit, you think?"

"For what? I'm not going anywhere. Not for a long time."

"Don't be silly. What have we been talking about? Plus, Rule Number Two of Being a Super Famous Person is—"

"—Be seen at all times—"

"—Especially in times of crisis. Right. Also, Danny wants to see you. So, let's pretty you up for your fiancé, okay?"

Ah, fuck.

Danny.

I'd forgotten all about him.

Chapter 4

This Is How You Build a Fairy Tale

So, you're probably asking yourself, How does a girl, even a shallow, disaster-actress girl like me whose long-term love just died, forget she has a fiancé?

And also, I'm sure, if she does have a fiancé, even one she forgets she has sometimes, what was she doing on that plane with Connor? What was she thinking?

The easy question first.

I don't have a fiancé. Not really.

Okay, maybe technically, but not really really.

Because I live in fantasyland, right? And this is how it works in fantasyland.

You're with a guy. I mean with with. Love-of-your-life, your-heart-beats-faster-every-time-you-see-him, you-act-like-a-different-person-around-him, love. But he keeps breaking your heart. You keep breaking his. You break each other's hearts. You don't know how to be together. You don't know how to be apart. You don't know how to be.

I mean, how do you be in love when the whole world's watching? When every fight, every drama, every moment of your togetherness is on display for the world to see? Is there a way? If there is, I never figured it out. I only succeeded in divorcing myself from reality for long enough that I mostly didn't notice that everyone was watching. But that was a temporary solution, which ended badly. Obviously.

So, I went to rehab. He went to rehab. We got back together, we left rehab, we broke up.

We continued this dance for the next year and a half. A Jane Austeny, Regency dance where we'd float together and almost touch but never quite make it. Well, of course we touched, but you know what I mean.

My heart was broken. My heart stayed broken.

Six months ago when he went on the bender to end all benders, I nearly threw my hard-won sobriety out the window to go along with him, but I was strong enough to end things instead. Taylor Swift style. We were never going to get back together, I told myself. Like never.

And my heart didn't matter anymore.

So there you are with your broken heart, and you've separated from the LOYL for what you tell yourself is the last time. The world is watching, and you're filming this (you're pretty sure) terrible movie with a boy/man, the boy/man of the moment, who's starring opposite you because the role calls for a super charming guy.

They've typecast him.

He is super charming.

You flirt on set. When he makes excuses to come see you in your trailer between takes, it makes you feel good. It makes you feel like you used to feel when you were with the LOYL, or when you took the drugs and alcohol you used to forget about him.

You flirt back. You touch his arm when you talk. You laugh harder at his jokes than might be called for, not because you're acting, but because it's easy to give in and laugh. It feels good. Nothing happens, not yet, but you both know it's only a matter of time.

Rumors escape from set. There's a photo taken of the LOYL surreptitiously checking out a tabloid that has a picture of you laughing with Super Charming Guy. Looking at the photo of the LOYL makes you feel good. Sad too, and, if you're being completely honest, a little maybe-this-will-bring-him-back.

But mostly, just good.

Then it's the wrap party. Everybody's drunk except for you and Super Charming Guy, who isn't drinking in "conspiracy" with you—that's what he says, and then he says, "All for one, and one for all," and you wonder if he knows what he's quoting from, or what the word "conspiracy" means. When he suggests that you "get the hell out of here," you nod and follow him out the back entrance, even though you know it's sure to be the lead story on *PerezHilton* tomorrow.

You think he's going to take you to his place, but he doesn't. Instead, because he's still in character, or maybe because he really is just a super charming guy, he drives you to the top of the hill that overlooks this crazy city you live in some of the time. You sit and watch the lights, the constant blurry traffic that never goes away no matter what time of night, and he confides in you. He tells you about his struggles to make it, how he was nervous to meet you, how he isn't nervous now, but he still kind of is, you know? And you nod, and put your hand on his arm. You kiss, and it feels nice. You kiss again and a flashbulb goes off.

An emergency summit is called.

After much debate, your respective publicists decide you have two weeks to date "privately." Two weeks where you'll tell anyone who asks that you're "just good friends," where you'll never be seen arriving anywhere together. During those two weeks he's still charming, he still makes you laugh, and when he kisses you and touches you and makes love to you, you can almost forget the LOYL.

Then the reprieve is up. It's time to go out into the light.

At the very first public event you attend together the questions start.

"Is it true you're moving in together?"

"Are you in love?"

"What's kissing Amber Sheppard like?"

And what can you say to these questions, but:

"That's a ways off yet."

"We're very happy."

"A gentleman doesn't tell."

"We're very happy," you repeat as you smile at one another on the red carpet. "It's too soon to talk about anything else."

It might be too soon for you, too soon for anyone normal or real, but you don't exist anywhere normal or real, and the questions keep coming. It doesn't take long before you're being referred to as an established item. "Long-term couple Amber Sheppard and Danny Garcia" starts to be the introduction to any story about you, like a month after that first kiss on the hilltop. They say you're living together, even though you aren't. That he's shopping for rings, though that can't possibly be true.

They stop talking about Camber, and start calling you Damber.

You're expected to answer to this name with a cutesy laugh.

You have to practice to get it right.

Another month later it's award season, and time speeds up. Neither of you have been nominated for anything, but you have a movie to promote, so you act like you have been. You attend every awards show there is and laugh like bells when the plasticized hosts say you're sure to be nominated next year.

Between the dieting and the working out and the trying on of dresses, you end up seeing him only at the events themselves, and the after-parties you should be skipping. At the Golden Globes, he gets asked for the first time when he's going to propose while you're standing right next to him, worried you'll faint from the juice fast that got you into the dress that was made for someone with the figure of an eleven-year-old girl.

He laughs it off, but by the Oscars he's started answering "Soon," and now it's your turn to laugh. That bell-ringing laugh you practiced but never got quite right.

That night, when you're sober again among the sea of drunken be-Oscared people, and he's tipsy because "you wouldn't mind, babe, right, if I had just one?" he pulls you out of the *Vanity Fair* party. He gets down on one knee right there among the topiaries and tells you that you've changed his life, asks you to be his wife.

You ignore the fact that this proposal came out in rhyme.

You don't say yes, but you don't say no, either.

You do, however, let him put a ridiculously large yellow diamond on your finger.

And when you work it out a couple of days later, you figure out that that night was just your twentieth date.

✪

Two hours later, Olivia ushers Danny into my apartment as if she's brokering a treaty between two warring nations.

I've showered and blow-dried and changed into a new lululemon outfit that looks exactly like the one I was wearing before only less rumpled. I can't remember the last time I didn't give a crap about what I was wearing or how I smelled. Okay, that's not true. I can remember, and I've spent years making sure I'd never be back there again, but here I am.

Olivia's cleaned up the traces of my meltdown. Fresh sheets are on the bed, blankets have been removed from the couch and folded, three Kleenex boxes and their former contents have been collected and thrown into the trash. The lights are on and the curtains are closed and there's music playing—Norah Jones, I think—just loudly enough that the *thawp* of the helicopter blades and the calls of the press are blurred, almost imperceptible.

Danny's wearing jeans that looked pressed, an Oxford shirt that plays up his greyish eyes, and—this is the part I have trouble forgiving him for—enough product in his hair to make it look like he's been running his fingers through it with worry.

"Amberina," he says as he pulls me against his chest.

Danny smells good and clean, and his arms are strong around me. I feel the tears start again, and I don't know what to do.

"It's okay, babe," he says, running his hand over my hair.

Babe, renkonti min . . .

Renkonti min . . .

Renkonti min . . .

Chapter 5

Twenty Questions

I guess I didn't answer the second question, did I? Why was I going to see Connor when I had a maybe fiancé? And also: why was I going to see Connor when I'd promised myself I wasn't ever going to see him again? Why couldn't I stop loving him despite everything?

These are heavy questions. I don't mean heavy like "that's heavy," said in a stoner voice. I mean heavy like weight. And that last question's been weighing me down almost since I met him.

I've never really known how to answer it. I mean, how do you explain breathing? Okay, I know there's a scientific explanation, but if you stop the average person on the street and you ask them how the body knows it needs to breathe every few seconds, even when it's asleep, they won't be able to explain it. Not really.

Autonomic response. Something that occurs involuntarily or spontaneously. Something you can't help. Something necessary. But if you break through that hard-wired barrier, if you start thinking too hard about breathing, then it can just stop. The only way it works is when you don't think about it.

That's what it felt like with Connor and me. That I didn't have any control over it, and that even if I tried to, I might end up not being able to breathe anymore.

And that's no way to live.

So the only answer I have after years of therapy and avoidance and asking myself *Why?* in the middle of the night is this.

There are people that are in your life whether you want them to be or not. Like family. Like skin. And for someone like that, you show up when they call. Even if you know it's a bad idea. Even if you know it will end badly, you show up eventually.

So that's what I was doing, out there on that ridiculous plane, on the runway. I was letting Connor know that even though we hadn't spoken for six months, I was still showing up for him when it mattered, that he was still a part of my skin.

But now I know that he didn't ask me to go to him because he really needed me. When he waggled his fingers as I was following him towards his suite and God knows what else, I realized he asked me because he knew he could get me to show up eventually. That he used our code, our special signal, without it meaning anything.

So I left, and he died, and now part of me is dead too.

But I showed up when he asked, even though I shouldn't have.

Even though it was bad for me.

I showed up, and he died anyway.

✪

"So," Olivia says after she's given Danny and me exactly five minutes alone. "What's the plan here?"

I wipe my hand across my eyes, smudging the mascara Olivia insisted I wear.

"Why do we need a plan?"

"Seriously, Amb?"

"Yeah."

"Well, first off, there's Rule Number Three of Being a Super Famous Person."

"I'm not sure I remember that one."

She rolls her eyes, as if she's told me a thousand times, which maybe she has.

"Get in front of the story."

"How do we do that?"

"Simple. Hold a press conference."

"A what?"

"A press conference. So you can answer everyone's questions instead of letting the rumor mill answer them for you."

Danny rubs small circles into my back. "I think that might be the way to go. They're never going to leave you alone unless you answer them."

Olivia's eyes narrow with her what-do-you-know-about-it? look. Although she brought him here, Olivia is not Danny's biggest fan. Then she realizes he's on her side.

She smiles approvingly. "See, Danny agrees. It's the way to go."

"Maybe you two should do it then."

"No one wants to talk to us, Amb."

"That's right," Danny says. "Just listen. They're asking for you."

He turns the knob on the stereo so the music's all the way off, and now I can hear it clearly. That drumbeat call.

Am-ber. Am-ber. Am-ber.

Another summons I'm going to have to answer, eventually.

The press conference takes place the next day at the Ritz-Carlton, Olivia's theory being that some of the hotel's respectability might wear off on me. Accordingly, I'm dressed in the most conservative outfit I've ever worn: a black shirtdress with a cleric's collar made of stiff fabric. It feels like a constant reminder to behave, but I feel so sick and weak and sad, I don't need to be reminded. I just have to get through this day, this hour, this minute, this second.

This second.

Danny stands with me in the wings while Olivia lays out the ground rules to the standing-room-only crowd. Amber can refuse to answer any question she wants. Amber will take only one question from each of the twenty people who were lucky enough to get a numbered card when they put their hand in the bingo wheel that she found I don't know where. We will be nice to Amber or we will be asked to leave and we will be placed on a list that no one wants to be on. That's right, Olivia's shit list.

~~I've actually seen this list. You do not want to be on it.~~

"Do we all understand the rules?" Olivia asks.

"Yes" comes the low chorus.

"All righty then, let the twenty questions begin."

Twenty questions is Olivia's favorite game. Downtime on the set, travelling places, any moment of silence is at risk of being filled by Olivia's insistence that we guess what she's thinking of in twenty questions or less.

Is that the end game here? Twenty questions and the world will know what I'm thinking?

Danny puts his hand on the small of my back. He whispers "Good luck," and leads me towards the simple table that sits on the stage. He and Olivia take seats on either side of me as the flashbulbs blind us with bright bursts of light.

"Question one!" Olivia barks.

A guy in his early forties who's been following me around for years stands up.

"Hey, Mike."

"Hi, Amber. I'm very sorry for your loss. We all are."

I feel Danny stiffen beside me. Letting him come was a mistake, but it didn't feel as if there was any other option when we discussed it briefly this morning. I mean, how do you leave out the guy you're supposedly engaged to from your grief about the guy you were trying to forget when you met him? Besides, his absence would just be something else for the press to speculate about, which we both knew without having to say it.

"Thank you. I . . . thank you."

"This has clearly been a big shock and a national tragedy. Everyone wants to know how you've been handling things, but can you tell us how you first found out about the crash?"

I close my eyes for a second, remembering the flash of images on the TV screen that were so hard to decipher and impossible to comprehend. "I saw it on television, actually."

"Question two!"

"Chris Butler here from ATV. We know you were on Connor's plane briefly, and that there's a video circulating of you jumping off it, which was filmed by one of the passengers. Why did you go see Connor that night?"

"Because he asked me to."

"Three!"

"Phyllis Hayes from *Starlet* magazine."

"I remember."

"Yes, um, well, anyway. This must have been a tough couple of days for you."

"Was that a question?" Olivia asks.

"No, um, sorry. Amber, coming back to the video of you jumping off the plane, what made you do that? Why were you in such a hurry to get off that flight?"

"I left because . . . I left because it wasn't a good scene for me."

"Because of the drugs?" a red-faced kid asks. "Is that what you mean, Amber? Was Connor doing drugs that night? Did you?"

Olivia leans towards her microphone. "We are supposed to wait until our number's called! Four!"

"I *am* number four," he says, his face now beet red. He looks younger than me.

"Last chance, people. Anyone else breaks the rules, this show's over. Proceed."

The red-faced kid tries again. "Was Connor doing drugs that night?"

"I couldn't say."

"Five!"

"Come on, Amber. Fess up," Mike's wife—Janice, Janet?—says. "You jumping off that plane isn't the only video from that night. Or are you telling us you haven't seen the footage which clearly shows Connor was drinking and using that night?"

I close my eyes. I know what she means, because one of those Orange Spray Tan girls *was* filming us, and it's been all over the Internet. The video starts a few minutes before I got on. There's the big bowl of white powder, then Connor's head bent over the table. It captures his look when he raised his head and saw me arrive. Then I walk into the shot. The camera closes in on my face. It's filled with a look of longing.

"Do you really expect us to believe Connor wasn't doing drugs that night?"

"Who said that?" Olivia growls snapping me out of it. She really missed her calling as an elementary school principal. "The perp better identify himself right now or we are done here."

I put my hand over my microphone. "'Perp'? Livvie. Come on."

"Rules are rules. I'm going to count to three. One . . ."

"Okay, okay," says a guy named Johnson, I think, or at least that's what I've heard him being called. It might also be a reference to his, you know. He's always trying to sleep with his prey, and sometimes he succeeds. "It was me."

Olivia crosses her arms. "We're waiting."

Johnson grumbles something I can't quite catch and stands. Everyone watches him as he shuffles towards the door. A couple of his competitors are smirking. Of course, he can now go file his story before they can, but I'm not about to mention that to Olivia.

"Six!" Olivia shouts when the doors clang shut behind him.

"He was six," Mike says, pointing over his shoulder.

"Seven!"

A woman who's sitting directly behind Mike coughs nervously

and stands. As my eyes connect with hers, I realize two things simultaneously: I'm looking at Katie Sandford, and I'm not going to like the question she has to ask.

"Hi, Amber."

"Hi, Katie."

A low murmur of recognition rumbles through the room. I met Katie in rehab, and she was "famous" for a bit herself after we got out.

Katie twists her chestnut hair around her finger. Her pale blue eyes are wide and clear. Sober.

"Quiet!" barks Olivia.

"I'm really sorry about Connor," Katie says.

"I know. Ask your question."

"I didn't want to do this."

"Just ask, okay?"

Her shoulders rise and fall with indecision, but she gets it out anyway.

"Who's the father of your baby?"

Chapter 6

Meet the Press

I made a friend in rehab. Her name was Katie, and while she wasn't as damaged as I was, she seemed to understand me. In fact, it was her very normalcy that drew me to her, I think. She knew who I was, but she didn't seem to care. She was struggling with her own thing, but she had time to help me with my struggle too. When Connor checked into our rehab facility with his best friend, Henry, in tow for some reason I still don't understand, she told me I didn't have to go to him when he called. And when I did anyway, she stayed on my side.

Finally, a friend, I remember thinking. A friendship that was about who I was, not what I was.

But here's the thing. She did care who I was. In fact, that was the whole reason she was in rehab. Katie was just pretending to be an alcoholic seeking help. Her real mission was me. She was sent there by a magazine called *Gossip Central* to befriend me. Get the inside scoop. Write an exposé. All to land her dream job as a music writer for *Gossip Central*'s sister magazine, *The Line*.

It turned out to be a piece of cake.

So, do I really have to say it?

I guess so.

No, I'm not pregnant. Not even a little bit.

But as I watch Kate shift uncomfortably from foot to foot with a room full of shocked eyes on her, looking like she wishes she could disappear, I start to get very, very angry.

CUT TO:
INT. HOTEL CONFERENCE ROOM--MOMENTS LATER

KATE SANDFORD (32), a journalist, chestnut hair,
light blue eyes, fit, pretty, and AMBER SHEPPARD
(25), petite, underfed, very much an actress, are
alone in the conference room where the press
conference took place. It's been emptied out.
Katie and Amber look small in the big, empty
room.

Amber's face is mottled with anger. Katie looks a
little frightened, but mostly ashamed.

                    AMBER
          Why would you think I was pregnant?

                    KATE
          There was a positive pregnancy test . . .
          in your garbage.

                    AMBER
          You've been going through my garbage?
          Seriously, Katie?

Kate looks at the floor.

                    KATE
          No, it wasn't me. I didn't do that.

                    AMBER
          Just someone at that ridiculous
          magazine, right? Why are you still
          doing their dirty work?

                    KATE
          The Line is owned by the same people as
          Gossip Central, you know that, and
          there was pressure on our editorial
          board and . . .

                    AMBER
          Unfuckingbelievable.

                    KATE
               (Speaking very quickly)
          I know this sounds like last time,
          okay. I get that. And it was that
          editor Bob's idea. We have to find a
          way to get more readers or we're all
          toast. Everyone's desperate, and --

                    AMBER
    So, if you get the inside scoop on my
    "pregnancy," then you get to keep your
    job?

                    KATE
    So you are pregnant?

                    AMBER
    No! But that's why you're asking,
    right?

                    KATE
    Well, yeah.

                    AMBER
    How is this not <u>exactly</u> like last time?

                    KATE
    (Beat) I promise I won't write about
    it?

    Kate looks at Amber sideways, waiting for her
    reaction.

    Amber's initially pissed off. Then starts to laugh.

                    AMBER
    I'll give you this, Katie. You've got
    balls.

✪

"How's Henry?" I ask Katie when I've stopped laughing and an uncomfortable silence has stolen over the room. "I mean, you guys are still together, right? I thought I heard that."

"Yeah, we are. And he's a complete mess."

"Because of Connor?"

"Of course because of Connor. Why else?"

"But they haven't spoken in years. They never made up after that fight, did they?"

Right after we got out of rehab, Connor pulled some crazy shit, and Henry actually took my side rather than Connor's. He quit working for Connor—even though he'd been his manager for years, and, I was pretty sure, never liked me—and he and Katie sort of saved my life that night, which is kind of an awesome thing to do for another person, when you think about it.

"No, they didn't," Katie says. "But what does that have to do with it? They grew up together. They were best friends for years. Besides, you haven't been with him for what, six months—a year?—and you're a mess . . ."

I look down at my hands.

"You are a mess, aren't you?" she asks. "Oh, Christ."

"What?"

"Are you on something right now?"

My head snaps up. "No! Why would you think that?"

"Because you just gave a press conference, and you looked pretty cool during it. Like medicated cool."

"Not that I owe you any explanations, Katie, and if you print this anywhere I'll end you, but this is the first time I've been outside my apartment since I heard the news. I couldn't even get out of bed until Olivia forced me out."

Katie shakes her head.

"What?"

"You'll 'end me'? Dramatic much?"

"Ah, fuck off."

She smiles a sad smile. "I've missed you. And I'm really sorry about Connor. About everything."

"Didn't keep you from taking the assignment, though, did it? Again."

"True. My name is Kate. I'm an alcoholic and an awful person."

"You have to really mean it when you say that."

"Ouch."

There's that silence thief again.

"There is one thing I don't understand," Katie says eventually.

"Only one thing?"

"Ha. Yeah. If you're not pregnant, why was there a positive pregnancy test in your trash?"

"Back to that, huh?"

"Back to that, but off the record, I promise. If that means anything to you."

I think about it. Do her promises mean anything to me? Can I trust her? Do I want to take the risk? But there's something else there too. Because how *did* that pregnancy test end up in my trash? Assuming Bob didn't plant it to manufacture a story, which I wouldn't put it past him to do.

Then I have a moment of clarity, as they call it in good ole AA.

And she must have one too, because when I meet Katie's eyes, we say it together.

"Olivia."

Chapter 7

Dealing out the Damage

Olivia did get my phone to stop ringing, all those years ago, after replacing my waterlogged one. The trick might've been as simple as changing my number and giving the press hers instead, but she did it. That, and whatever else I needed since. Along the way, I grew to trust her. She knew the worst things about me, but she never judged. Truth be told, she participated in the worst sometimes, but back then that was one of the things I liked about her.

God, we had fun sometimes, you know? Olivia always knew how to produce fun, no matter what Podunk town I was shooting in that month. (A little-known fact: Movies with roman numerals in their names are shot almost exclusively in Podunks.) Like this one time, we were shooting in Washington State and we had a down day because we were supposed to shoot exteriors and it was raining (again). Olivia packed me into her car, and a couple of hours later we were in Forks. As in the *Twilight* books. Maybe you didn't know, but the book is based on an actual town, with an actual Indian reservation nearby, and that town's been given over entirely to *Twilight* kitsch.

Connor and I had this whole thing about *Twilight*. We always told people we hated it but, really, I'd read all the books in two weeks, imagining us as Bella and Edward. Well, okay, I did a little more than imagine it. It's a well-guarded secret that we were actually supposed to have been cast in the roles, but then Connor failed a drug test and I pulled out because I didn't want to do it without him.

Yes, I actually turned down that role because of Connor.

How stupid can one person be?

The best part of Forks was a store called Dazzled by Twilight. Apparently, there were actually two of these stores in the town at one time. Two. Anyway, it was a weird mix of store and haunted house where Olivia and I took pictures of ourselves next to life-sized cardboard cutouts of Edward and Bella. We laughed so hard our sides hurt for days afterwards.

That place burned down a couple of years ago. Olivia sent me a link to the story about it with one of the pictures we took that day. Only she'd digitally manipulated Connor's face over Edward's, so it looked like we were posing on either side of him, ready to bite his skin, which shone bright like a diamond in the sun.

✪

Danny's very quiet on the ride back to my apartment.

Usually, he's a chatterbox, an endless flow of quips and one-liners and energy, but today he just stares straight ahead as if he's looking at a manifestation of the word "fatherhood," and that word is synonymous with "terrified" and "no way."

But we're not alone in the car—there is the potentially curious driver to consider—and so I have to wait to say anything until we pass the thrumming crowd outside my building and are finally in the relative quiet of my apartment.

"It's not true," I say, taking his hands and leading him to the couch.

"What now?"

"I'm not pregnant. I wasn't pregnant. It's not true."

He drops my hands. "Of course."

"So you don't have to worry, okay?"

He smiles sadly. "Really?"

"No."

"Come on, Amb. I know you think I'm dumb, but I'm not. I'm really not."

"What do you mean?"

"You were with Connor the night he died. After everything he did to you. Despite us."

"But . . . you already knew that, didn't you?"

"When you were talking with Katie, I watched the video from the plane. Like, really watched it . . ."

"I don't understand."

"The look you gave Connor when you saw him. You've never looked at me like that."

"Oh."

He reaches towards my left hand and captures the enormous yellow diamond between his thumb and forefinger.

"Did this . . . did I ever mean anything? To you?"

"Of course you did. I mean, you do."

He mumbles, "The truth will out . . ."

"If you had your eyes, you might fail of the knowing me: it is a wise father that knows his own child."

"Excuse me?"

"That's the rest of the quote."

"What are you talking about?"

"'The truth will out,' it comes from *The Merchant of Venice*."

"How do you know that?"

"Stupid party trick."

"Are we really talking about Shakespeare right now?"

"No, I'm sorry."

"Can you just tell me what's going on?"

I pull my hand away from him and tuck my knees up under my chin "Truth?"

"That's what I'm asking."

"He'd been texting me for days, months really, wearing me down. That day he was texting me every hour and I thought . . . I thought it was something important. But then I got there and I saw . . . you saw what I saw, so I left."

"Did you use?"

"No."

"Is this the first time you've seen him since we've been together?"

"Yes."

"But not the first time you've been in touch with him?"

"He . . . writes me sometimes," I say, not bothering to correct the tense this time. Just the thought of it is sucking the light out of the room. "He writes to me, but I don't write back."

"I wish I could believe that."

"I don't know what to tell you. It's true."

"You still love him though, right?"

"I've loved him since I was fifteen."

"How am I supposed to compete with that?"

I search his face, this adorable man who's been like a puppy in my life, all cuddly enthusiasm, and he looks so different I almost don't recognize him. "I don't want you to try. You shouldn't have to."

"You're right, I shouldn't."

"But I can't change that. Just like I can't change the fact I'm an addict or all the stupid things I've done. I can't change how I feel about Connor or what he's been in my life. I can only be accountable for the future."

"Who are you quoting this time?"

He really is much smarter than I've ever given him credit for. And maybe this man, *this* man, is someone I could love for real, out in the daylight instead of under the spotlight.

But I've screwed it up. Just like I screw everything up eventually.

At least he's getting out of here alive.

"I don't even know," I say. "I've been fed so much of this stuff over the years, I don't know the difference between what someone else told me and what I've come up with on my own. But it's true, and it's what's kept me sober."

"Yet you were willing to risk all that, to risk us, because Connor asked you to meet him?"

Babe, renkonti min . . .

Babe, renkonti min . . .

"Yes, I guess I was."

He stands up. "Thanks for being honest."

"Are you leaving?"

"Yeah. You know."

"Forever?"

"I think that's best. You're not going to fight for me, are you? You're not going to fight for us."

"I'm sorry, I don't think I have any fight left."

He nods like he knew what I was going to say before I did, and leaves without another word. I stay on the couch, half rocking, listening to the buzz outside grow and grow as Danny exits the building.

Danny, are you and Amber still getting married?

Is it your baby, Danny?

Do you still love her?

Dan-ny. Dan-ny. Dan-ny.

"Don't leave me," I say to the empty room ten minutes too late and unsure of whether I'm talking to Danny, or Connor, or myself.

✪

I'm still on the couch an hour later when the buzzing gets louder again and *Oli-vi-a. Oli-vi-a. Oli-vi-a* is at my door.

"Well, this is a complete clusterfuck," she says. "I thought the press conference would calm things down. Obviously, I didn't count on Katie-Turncoat-Sandford turning up. What Henry sees in her, I'll never know."

Olivia and Henry used to date, and she pretty much hated Katie on sight, even before the whole she-followed-me-into-rehab-to-get-the-inside-scoop thing became public.

"How did it happen, Livvie?"

"I knew she was going to be trouble the minute I saw her there. I should've had her thrown out."

"Not Katie. The pregnancy thing."

She gives me a quizzical look. "I don't have to explain the birds and the bees to you, do I?"

"Come on. You know I'm not pregnant, so how did that pregnancy test get in my trash? Did you put it there? Some kind of publicity stunt? Some Rule of Being a Super Famous Person I don't know about?"

Her eyes widen in shock, but there's a reason Olivia's my publicist and not the actress she's always wanted to be.

"Do you honestly think I'd do that? After all this time?"

"Honestly? Yes. If you thought it was going to serve some purpose. Is that it? You thought if people believed I was pregnant and I 'lost' the baby, they'd be nicer to me for a while?"

"No, I—"

"—That's it, isn't it?"

Her hand flutters to her stomach briefly. "No, Amber, I swear, that's not it."

"What I can't understand," I continue, barely listening to her, "is how you got your hands on a positive pregnancy test. Is that something you can order online these days?"

She walks to the couch and sits down, pale, pale, pale.

"Maybe it wasn't your trash," she says flatly.

"*Gossip Central* wouldn't make that kind of rookie mistake. They would've been totally damn sure before they sent Katie in there to ask the question. So what the fuck, Livvie? What the fuck?"

"Will you please calm down?"

"I'm finding it kind of hard to calm down right now, okay? Will you just tell me what's going on?"

"It was mine, all right?"

"What?"

"It's mine. It was my test."

"You're pregnant?"

She hangs her head. "Yeah."

"Why didn't you tell me?"

"I only found out for sure a week ago, and then all this happened . . ."

"But . . . if it's your test, why was it in my garbage?"

"I did the test here. I used my key."

"Why?"

"Because I didn't want Chris finding it, if it was positive."

Chris is her live-in boyfriend.

"But you guys have been together for a while now. He's great. Does he not want kids?"

She brings her hands to her face, not caring about smudging her veneer of makeup, and this uncharacteristic gesture hits home, knocking the obtuseness right out of me.

"Chris isn't the father?"

"No," she whimpers miserably.

"Jesus, Livvie."

"It was just one time. Oh, that sounds so stupid. Like all those stories you told me from rehab. But it *was* just one time. One stupid time when Chris was on a business trip a couple of months ago . . ."

"Did you tell him?"

"No, of course not."

"What are you going to do?"

"I don't know. Before all this, I probably wasn't going to keep it, but now, I feel like I owe it to him, you know?"

"Owe it to Chris?"

"No."

"To who, then?"

"To Connor," she says quietly.

Numbing shock spreads through me as my mind skips and

whirls towards the truth.

Olivia's head sinks to her knees and she's sobbing now, loud, heaving sounds of grief, and she doesn't have to say the words for me to know.

She slept with Connor.

And she's pregnant with his baby.

Chapter 8

We Are Gathered Here Today

Connor's parents never liked me.

Not even in the beginning, when I was America's sweetheart and everyone wanted me living next door to them.

I don't know why. They're solid, smallish-town folks, but it's not like I came from some super rich background. I wasn't any different from Connor, really. And I certainly tried hard enough. The first time Connor took me home, I brought a hostess gift and I slept in his childhood bed while he slept on the couch, and we didn't even try to sneak him into my room. I ate way more than I normally do at dinner, helped clean up afterwards, and was super polite. But his mother just watched me with her mouth drawn in a thin line, and his father answered my questions as if the police were grilling him.

I spent a lot of time, off and on, trying to figure out what it was. Did they not want us together because Connor was older than me? That seemed to bother the press a lot—Cradle Robber became Connor's forename for a while—but I wasn't the one doing something wrong by dating him, if it was wrong. Or was it because of the partying? Connor was doing that long before I met him, and while it got worse when we were together, it's not like they knew that was going to happen, not that first time, six weeks in, as I sat with my napkin on my lap being as dainty as I could with his mom's homemade spaghetti.

There were a lot of becauses that never led anywhere. But when the shit hit the fan, when I fell apart and Connor fell apart and we fell radically apart, there his parents' faces were.

And their unified look said *I told you so*.

✪

Connor's funeral. A large, white church not big enough to hold the crowd of A- and B-list stars who've come to pay their last respects, though many of them never respected him in life, and many more never even knew him in life.

Crowds of his fans, three deep, line the blocks leading to the church. They're being held back by yellow caution tape and bored-looking policemen. Long lines of limos disgorge their black-clad cargo onto the red carpet that someone was tasteless enough to drape over the stairs. There are cameras and cameramen and professional lighting, but at least no one is posing for pictures.

Not obviously, anyway.

Though I received many, *many* calls from designers who wanted to "dress me for the occasion," I'm wearing an old black dress I've had for years. It isn't flashy. It isn't Hollywood. It's something Katie would wear, and in fact, it's very similar to what she is wearing. My face is makeup-free, and my hair is in a conservative knot at the base of my neck. I left the yellow diamond behind, and instead I'm wearing the first and only piece of jewelry Connor ever gave me, a small platinum heart on a simple chain that once belonged to his mother, and to his grandmother before that.

When I climb out of my limo, I get my first surprise of the day. The press stays silent. There's only the *click, click, click* of shutters. I bite my bottom lip to keep it from quivering and let an usher guide me up the stairs.

Inside the church now. Long rows of uncomfortable wooden pews. A stained-glass window at the end of the aisle, all prismed sunlight colors. Connor's cousins handing out programs. Black-clad security guards leading people to their assigned seats, the Hollywood hierarchy established by some ancient code I've never been able to crack.

Olivia would know. Only I'm not talking to Olivia.

Connor's parents—who have, not surprisingly, not been taking my calls—are in the front row. His mother's sitting in an erect daze that must be the effect of some of the same drugs she condemned us for using. She was right to do that, of course, and if I didn't think it would start me down a road that would lead to my own funeral, I'd be doped to the gills myself.

And what doesn't any of it matter, really?

Their son is dead.

I'm still alive.

That's enough for them, apparently.

I've been allowed to attend the funeral, to be seated halfway down the left-hand side aisle, but I'm not allowed to speak. Bernard told me so this morning at my apartment when I was trying to decide if this one day at time was one day too many. He's been in "fucking negotiations" with Connor's agent for days without me knowing, and there are "more conditions than for your insurance bond, but the upshot is: you can go."

"They didn't even want me to go to the funeral?"

"They're very angry."

"But *I* wasn't flying the plane. I wasn't even supposed to be on the plane. And if I'd stayed, I would've died too. I know they hate me but . . ."

Bernard sighed. "Apparently, he told them he was leaving treatment to try to get you back."

"He was in treatment again? When?"

"A couple of months ago. They managed to keep it hush-hush, though I don't know how."

Oh, God. Oh no. A couple of months ago. When he started texting me again. When he somehow—how, how, how?—ended up sleeping with Olivia.

When I got engaged.

"I didn't know any of this." I sank to the floor. "I did this. I did this."

Bernard grabbed me by the elbow roughly. "Stop that right this minute. You didn't do shit. If that dumb ass left treatment on some stupid quest to win you back when he never deserved you in the first place, that's his goddamn problem. And none of that had anything to do with his plane going down. That was just a bad bit of random. You listening to me?"

"Yes."

"Good. You've got to keep it together, okay? I couldn't stand . . . you've got to make it, Amber."

He hugged me to him and I rested my head on his shoulder. He's the closest thing I've had to a father for a long time, and I realized I'd never told him that. How important he was to me.

"I love you, Bernard."

"I love you too, kid. Now, enough of this shit. Olivia find you something appropriate to wear?"

"I'll manage."

He nodded and left me to get ready, and somehow I did.

Katie and Henry are sitting a few rows ahead of me. I force myself not to search the room for Olivia. If she's here, she's the last person I want to see.

Henry turns his head, and I can see what Katie said is true. He's a complete mess. He's so pale he looks ill, and red blotches spot his cheeks.

I can't believe I questioned his grief.

I am the worst. The worst.

The funeral's a bit of a fog after that. I listen to the first minute of his father speaking, but I have to tune it out or I'll scream. Instead, I concentrate on counting down from a thousand in my head.

Surely that will be long enough for this to be over?

At 273, 272, 271, Henry stands, a notebook clutched in his hand, and I stop counting. He climbs to the podium and searches the crowd. As his eyes meet mine, my hand rises reflexively to the heart at my throat. Henry nods his head slightly and starts to speak.

"My name is Henry Slattery. Connor and I met in elementary school and we grew up together. We went through all the stuff that boys do. Trucks and fights and video games and girls. All that stuff. I guess you're expecting me to say, like some others have, that there was always something special about Connor, that we all knew back then he'd be this big star. Clearly, none of you have seen a picture of what Connor looked like before he turned sixteen."

Everyone laughs, and Henry pauses to take a sip of water. I smile too as I remember those pictures, still hanging in his parents' house. They fascinated me the first time I saw them. His features all grew at different times, and he had braces and acne. He looked like such a . . . such a dork, it was hard to believe the transformation.

"What he did have, though," Henry continues, "what he always had, was this enormous sense of unpredictable adventure. It was infectious, and I think that's why he made it. If I had to pick one thing. People connected with him, even through a screen, because of that impulsive wildness. You just had to watch and see what he was going to do next.

"I guess most of you know I was his manager for a while. We didn't see much of each other after high school, though we kept in touch as best we could. I went to college; he got famous. Then he called and asked me to come be a part of it. 'You can't *not* come,' he said, and he was right. I couldn't say no to him. Not for a long time. Not many people could."

He pauses and looks at me again.

"It's no secret that he had trouble saying no to himself. He acted like he was invincible, but it was an act. He was too damn stubborn to ever really ask for help. I waited and I waited for him to ask, to really mean it, but he never did. So I finally said no to him, and we haven't spoken since. I'll question every day if I made the right decision, as I have every day since I made it. And even though it wasn't the drugs that killed him in the end, I'm sure there are many people in this room who're asking themselves if they could've done something so he wouldn't have been on that plane, on that day, at that time. One more phone call? One more email? One more speech about how he owed it to himself to do better?

"I know someone else in this room is asking herself that most of all. But Amber, the answer is no. We did what we could. We did our best."

I keep on staring at Henry as a roomful of eyes turn towards me as one. I can feel their weight on me, their accumulated expectations.

Henry raises his fist to his cheek, wiping away a tear.

"You know, it's funny. One of the things I've been thinking about these last couple of days is how the two people in the world who are probably going to miss him the most besides his folks weren't really in his life anymore. And one of the saddest things for me is it means that some of my memories of him are already a little faded, a little worn.

"Funerals are supposed to be a time of healing, and I believe that. Just like I know that, whatever his flaws, Connor loved with his whole heart, and he lived that way too. For good or bad. We can't change that about him, and now we have to stop trying."

He turns towards the enormous picture of Connor next to him—frozen full-of-life laughter on his twenty-five-year-old face. How he looked when I met him. How he looked when I loved him most.

"I love you, brother. Wherever you are, I hope you know that now. I'll miss you forever."

His voice cracks, and he leaves the stage paler than ever. And though everyone expects him to go to Katie, I know like there's a cord connecting us that he's coming to me. So I stand and wait, and when he gets to me we collapse onto each other, letting it all out, not caring who sees.

"He knows," I say to Henry. "He's always known."

Chapter 9

On the Outside Looking In

When I was sixteen, I got legally emancipated from my parents. This meant they weren't managing me anymore, and though I knew I needed some kind of representation because my contract with *TGND* was in the middle of being renegotiated, and even sixteen-year-old me wasn't arrogant enough to conduct my own contract negotiations, I wasn't in any hurry to find a replacement.

When the news of the split with my parents came out, I'd been swamped with calls from breathless assistants trying to set up lunch meetings, and then from senior assistants, and finally from a host of brash agents who tried all kinds of approaches to get me to be their next meal ticket. But none of their various versions of "I have your best interest at heart," ever rang true, and eventually they stopped calling. Of course, that also meant I wasn't getting sent many scripts anymore. Or at least, nothing that wasn't some remake of a 1980s Disney movie.

Connor kept telling me, "Just use my agent, baby. He'll hook you up," but for some reason I resisted until Connor passed me the phone one morning and his agent was on the line, telling me about the "perfect part." He sent over the script and I read it and it *was* perfect. The movie was called *When You're Gone*, and the role was a young woman whose father had disappeared ten years before, leaving her, her mother, and her little brother behind. She'd always chosen to believe he was dead, but it turns out he was just an asshole, because he comes back and tries to repair their relationship and . . . oh, I'm not doing it justice, but the whole heart of the story was this father-daughter thing, and the dialogue was perfect, you know, like real conversations, and I read the script three times in two days. I studied and studied for the audition, even dialed down the partying for a week, and I went into the room and I nailed it.

Or I thought I had until I read in *Variety* a week later that the part had gone to Kimberley Austen, my . . . what's that word for people who kind of get everything you've always wanted? . . . nemesis. And Connor was going to be her love interest and . . . anyway, it sucked to want something that badly and not get it, and I kind of knew that part of the reason I didn't get it was because I didn't have anyone advocating for me.

A few weeks later, Bernard turned up on the set of *TGND*. He repped one of our directors, and he'd somehow got ahold of my audition tape for *When You're Gone*. He sat me down and played it, explaining what had worked in my audition and what had not. Then he froze the frame on this one moment, this sort of shy, angry look I was giving, and he said, "You and I are going to make a lot of money together."

And that's what we did.

★

I spend the next week of my life hiding. Hiding from the press. Hiding from my cravings. Hiding from life. But I also spend a lot of time investigating.

Or maybe that's not the right way to describe it. Is reading everything that's been written about you over the last several years "investigating"? Maybe the right word is "ruminating".

Whatever it is, that's what I do. Because given everything, I can't help but wonder. How would I see myself from the outside, looking in? What does my life really look like? How far from reality has it flown?

So I read the articles about me, and watch the videos, and scroll through years of back posts on *TMZ* and *PerezHilton* and *Us Weekly*, and ignored all texts and calls and emails from Olivia. By the end of it, through my scratchy eyes and fogged brain, I feel like I can finally see it. My life, for what it really is.

And it isn't pretty.

★

"I want to do something about it," I say to Bernard when I've read it all, seen it all, relived it all.

"What do you want to do?"

We're in the boardroom in his office, which he keeps at a

temperature slightly above that of a meat locker, and I'm shivering like I'm two days into detox. Which maybe I am, if you can detox from yourself.

"I want to fix it. I want . . . myself back."

Bernard paces around the room, ignoring the breathtaking view of the city. I've often wondered why he pays for what must be extremely expensive real estate. He doesn't care about it, and nobody books his clients because he has a great office view.

It's more of a fear-factor kind of thing.

"Well, I can probably translate all this into some sympathy auditions. There's that biopic they're casting for . . . What's her fucking name? The shower girl."

"Shower girl?"

"You know. The knife, the music. Eueueue." He makes as if to stab me as he brays the theme from *Psycho.*

"You mean Janet Leigh?"

"Right. Her. You can pull off bleached blonde, right?"

I shudder at the thought of it, my scalp already tingling.

"Or a wig. Whatever."

"I'm not talking about auditions. I'm talking about my life. I want it back."

He rounds on me. "You want to fucking quit on me? Now?"

"No, I just . . . I want to be able to leave my condo without caring if I'm having a good hair day, without having to wear sunglasses because otherwise they might get a shot of me with my eyes half closed because I'm blinking and so I look drunk. I want to have a real relationship with a real person—"

"—You want to be a citizen."

"Citizen" is his contemptuous term for anyone outside the business.

"No, I want to be . . . Jennifer Garner. Doesn't she have a pretty normal life? Or Harrison Ford?"

"Harrison Ford owns half of Wyoming. You want to do that? You want to buy half of the fucking Dakota Territory? Build a little house on the prairie?"

"Didn't the Dakota Territory become Idaho mostly?"

"Don't be a show-off."

"Okay, okay, but will you work with me here, Bernard?"

"So you're saying you're going to work like Jennifer Garner now?

Professional. No drama. Letting her husband take the spotlight. Three kids?"

"Come on, Bernard. It's not like I haven't been trying."

"Yeah, it kind of *is* like that, though."

"Ouch."

"Sorry, kid, but it's true."

"So what do I have to do, then? For real?"

Bernard gets this gleam in his eye. "I've been waiting a lifetime to hear you ask that."

★

It turns out Bernard's plan is very simple and—I can attest to this because it's been in action for a week—very, very boring.

"Do nothing," he says.

"Like nothing nothing?"

"Nothing interesting. You've heard about Madonna, right?"

"I've heard a lot of things about Madonna."

"Well, no actually, you haven't. You only hear about Madonna when she wants you to. And she does that by doing nothing."

I wasn't completely sure about this. I mean, that whole cheating on her cute British Director Husband with A-Rod, did she want that to come out? That was definitely doing something.

"You're going to have to explain this to me."

"Take her clothes. She wears the same thing. Every. Fucking. Day. As a result, no photograph of her is worth anything because it looks just like any other photograph. She applies this philosophy to most of her life. And as a result, if you're hearing about Madonna, it's because she wants your attention."

"But hasn't she been wearing a grill, lately? And those weird gloves to cover her old hands? I mean, I guess she wears those every day, so it's kind of right, but—"

"—Will you just work with me here?"

"So you're saying . . . bore them to death and they'll go away until I have something un-boring to say?"

"Exactly. You're going to need a routine."

"Like a schedule?"

"Like you're in training for the Olympics."

"Um, okay. What do I have to do?"

"For starters, you'll get up at eight every day."

"Eight! In the morning?"

"Of course in the morning. Do you want the plan to work or not?"

"Okay, okay. What else?"

"You will eat breakfast."

"Bernard."

"You will eat breakfast so that people hear that you are eating breakfast and they will see you put on a little weight."

"You want me to get fat."

"I want you to get healthy. You're looking skeletal, even for you. So, you'll eat something boring like muesli and half a grapefruit. And take some vitamins while you're at it."

"You're killing me."

"I'm saving you. Next. You'll do your own hair so it looks okay but not glamorous. You'll dress in ordinary clothes. Jeans. Simple shirts. Gap, Old Navy, that kind of shit. You'll wear sunglasses only when absolutely necessary."

"Anything else?"

"I'm just getting started. You'll work out once a day, preferably the same routine, with a trainer. Running, hiking, Pilates, whatever, your choice."

"Gee, thanks."

He smiled. "You're welcome. You're also going to have lunch every day, someplace simple, like a sandwich shop, with a friend."

"Which friend?" I asked, fearing he was going to say 'Olivia.'

"No one you've seen in years, that's which friend. Start with the cast from *The Girl Next Door*. Reconnect with them. Writers, directors, fucking key grips. All I care about is that you have a normal, alcohol-free lunch every day. Outside, where they can see you."

"What if those guys won't have lunch with me? Some of them…"

At some point during *The Girl Next Door's* five-year run, I may have become a nightmare on set. Maybe.

"They'll come, if only out of curiosity."

"What are we going to talk about, me and the key grips?"

"Old times, of course. Exclusively."

"Awesome."

"Talk about things normal people talk about. Their families, the projects they're working on, that kind of shit. Make it about them, not about you."

"And if—when—they ask about me, what am I supposed to say?"

He cocks his hip and makes as if to flip his hair over his shoulder, a parody of one of TGND's signature moves. "You're, like, totally sad about Connor, but you're just trying to work through things, you know, like get your life back on track—"

I whack him in the arm. "I don't talk like that. Do I?"

"Not usually. Anyway, you get the idea."

"I'm starting to."

"Good. In the afternoons, you'll volunteer."

"Oh, come on. No one's going to fall for that."

"You will volunteer. Animal shelter, homeless shelter, library, whatever you want. Every day."

"Are you trying to make me fall off the wagon?"

"Of course not. Anyway, you'll be going to meetings every night, so no danger of that happening."

"A dream come true. Why don't you just send me back to rehab?"

"I thought about that, but you've used up all your rehab credit. We need to go more drastic."

"More drastic than sending me to rehab when I don't need to go?"

"I'm talking you-joined-Scientology-and-are-working-your-way-up-the-bridge-to-total-freedom-looking-for-Xenu drastic. Without, you know, the Scientology part."

"How long do I have to keep this up?"

"Until it works."

It only works if you work it. Is there an AA slogan for everything?

"Define 'works.'"

"Until people stop laughing when I call them and tell them you'd be perfect for a part in their movie."

"Again, ouch."

"You've got to toughen up."

"So, how long is this going to take?"

"How long between when you met Danny and you got engaged?"

"Three months."

"That sounds about right."

✪

I've been following Bernard's plan. I get up every day and work out with my trainer and eat a bland breakfast and take my vitamins. I haven't had a blow out in a week, though I did have to buy new clothes—purchased for me by Bernard's assistant—because nothing in my wardrobe was tame enough for him. None of my new clothes fit me properly, and I've gained three pounds. I'm starting to look healthy, which had better stop pretty soon if I ever want to get cast in anything again.

I've also been volunteering at the local actor's studio, giving lessons to kids who can't afford to pay for the program, and I've been to seven meetings in seven days. I've also had seven remember-that-time-when-blah-blah-blah lunches, and have turned out my light at 10 p.m. on the dot seven nights in a row. I've read three books and twenty scripts, and I've never been so bored in my entire life.

It hasn't all gone according to plan. The acting classes were met in the press with complete derision—*Who does she think she is, teaching other people to act? She shouldn't be allowed near children!* etc., etc.—my Oscar nomination for *Northanger Abbey* long forgotten. And though I check each morning, counting carefully, the number of people waiting outside my door has not diminished.

The prevailing sentiment seems to be: *How long can she keep this up?* And: *We clearly need to be there when she loses it.* And also: *She's obviously pregnant. Why else would she be treating herself so well?*

But buried in among all the negativity there's also this: *Is she turning over a new leaf?* And this: *I've always been rooting for her!* And also: *We're so proud of her!* (This last one might have been written by the head of the Amber Sheppard fan club, who's kind of been semi-stalking me for most of my life. But hey, I'll take it.)

It all might've worked eventually. If I could've stood it, if I could've kept it up.

But then something happens that brings it all crashing down.

Danny goes on Cathy Keeler.

Chapter 10

Confess, Confess

"Tell us, Danny, are you still engaged to Amber Sheppard, yes or no?" Cathy Keeler asks, like she's Oprah getting a doping confession from Lance Armstrong.

"No," Danny says, assuming a penitent pose.

They're sitting on Cathy Keeler's "confession dais," as it's generally referred to. This is where the notorious and famous come to confess their sins and—if tough-as-nails Cathy decides to grant absolution—to be forgiven. I had my own turn on the dais after I got out of rehab, back when I still thought confession was good for the soul/career. It didn't work out that way, obviously. And I'm guessing this episode isn't going to do wonders for my career either.

"Is she pregnant with your child, yes or no?"

"No."

The audience of fifty-something women leans in. Danny's speaking slowly, quietly as if he's on some kind of sedative.

Cathy Keeler's bottle-red hair shines under the bright arc lights. Her matching red nails are a tad short of talon length. "So then, Danny, I have to ask. Were you ever a real couple or was this all just some publicity stunt?"

"Things were real for me. You'd have to ask Amber how she felt."

"Now, come on, Danny, you must have some idea?"

"I think maybe she was just using me."

Someone in the audience emits a shocked *tsk*. Cathy Keeler, on the other hand, looks like she isn't shocked at all. And no doubt she isn't, given how she's always expecting the worst, and teaching her audience of millions to do the same.

Oh, Danny. Please don't do this.

"Now, I know this might be a bit hard for you to talk about, but did you ever see Amber drink or use drugs?"

Danny covers his eyes with his hand like the question hurts him.

He's a much better actor than I've ever given him credit for.

"Yes," he says.

"Yes? Both?"

He lowers his hand and nods.

"You've seen her use drugs? Was it crack again?"

"I'd rather not say," he answers. And by saying that, he's essentially confirming it.

The giant screen behind him flickers and there I am, sucking on a crack pipe in the video that was viewed by millions within days of its release. I've never allowed myself to watch it, but I remember the night like it was yesterday. I don't need a video to remind me of the dank room, the awful smells, the way my heart felt as if it would explode. The way I knew I might be dying and I didn't even care.

The camera pans to the audience smiling warmly at Danny, their approval clear. Such a good, honest boy, led astray but such a bad, bad girl.

Everyone knows Cathy Keeler only talks to victims.

"Danny, do you think Amber was still secretly dating Connor Parks while you were together?"

He hesitates. "She was still in love with him, yes."

"Did you know she was seeing him that night?"

"No."

Danny looks miserable, and Cathy Keeler reaches out to take his hand. The audience holds its collective breath. Everyone knows what's coming.

"So tell us, Danny, why have you come on the show tonight?"

"Because I . . . I want Amber to get help. I still care for her and..." He hangs his head in shame. And it might be real. Maybe Cathy Keeler's his rehab from me, and when the stage lights dim, he'll be able to walk away clean, leaving me behind.

There's a *click* and the sounds goes off.

"Well, this is fan-fucking-tastic," Bernard says, throwing the remote aside. "Fan. Fucking. Tastic. Seriously, Amber, if you tried harder, I don't think you could fuck this up any worse."

"I could get caught smoking crack again," I say in a slightly hopeful tone. Not because I want to smoke crack, at least not today, but because I'm worried Bernard's going to have a heart attack if he doesn't calm down, and I can't remember how to perform CPR.

"Oh, would you, please? That'd be a huge help."

"You've got to relax, Bernard."

"Sure, right. Relax."

He holds his hand to his chest and breathes in and out through his nose.

"Are you okay? Do I need to call an ambulance?"

"I'm having a heart attack, but not, you know, of the medical kind."

"Jeez, Bernard."

"Since you're the cause of it, you should be a tiny bit more sympathetic."

"You can blame me for a lot of things, but not this, okay? He's the one who broke up with me. I obviously had no idea he was going to go on Cathy Keeler and tell the world about it."

"What is that little bastard thinking?"

"He's hurt."

"Yeah, so, go drink yourself into a stupor or tell it to your therapist. You don't go on Cathy Keeler and lie about my client."

Now it's my turn to look at the floor. "He didn't lie."

"Excuse me?"

"He was telling the truth. Mostly."

"So you're telling me you're drinking again? Doing drugs?"

"No."

"Then what the—"

"—One time, at his house, after an awards show, I woke up and my back went into a complete spasm. Probably because of these crazy heels I was wearing. Anyway, he gave me something. He said it was a muscle relaxant, but when he gave me the bottle, I could tell it wasn't over-the-counter. I was in so much pain I didn't ask what it was, and I didn't care. But that's the only time since I left the Oasis. I swear."

"And the drinking?"

"His parents threw us an engagement dinner, and they were toasting us with champagne, and everyone was saying things like, 'Oh, come on, Amber, one little sip of champagne can't hurt.' It felt like some kind of test. You know, could she have just one sip and nothing more? I was so sick of it, and I wanted his parents to like me, so I did it and I smiled for the picture, and then I went to the bathroom and spat it out."

"You're telling me there's a picture of you with a champagne glass at your lips?"

"His sister has it. But she wouldn't—"

"—We have no idea what she would or wouldn't do. What about the rest of it? And where's Olivia? Why isn't she here dealing with this shit?"

"We're not speaking."

"Brilliant. Do I even want to know?"

"I don't even want to know."

"Moving on."

"I wasn't with Connor when I was with Danny, but I was still in love with him, of course I was. I'll always be in love with him."

He looks like he's about to launch into another speech, then stops as something on the television catches his attention. Danny's finished with his confessional, and now Cathy Keeler's posed in front of a screen filled with private photographs of my life. I have a bad feeling in the pit of my stomach. I grab the remote and turn up the volume.

" . . . I was contacted today by Amber Sheppard's parents. They have some *shocking* revelations to share, so tune in tomorrow. You definitely don't want to miss tomorrow's show."

Bernard tips his head into his hands. "My plan, my beautiful plan."

My life. My lost, lost life.

Chapter 11

Just a Little Bit of History Repeating

I hate my fucking parents.

That sounds harsh. That sounds ungrateful. But listen.

When I was four years old, I told my mom I wanted to be in the movies. And though this wasn't something she ever thought about before, my mother is someone who knows how to get things done when she sets her mind to it. She's also the kind of person who tries to make her four-year-old's dreams come true. She was, anyway.

So off I was sent for lessons and headshots and auditions, and I was happy as a clam. I modeled in local catalogues of kids' clothes, did a couple of commercials, basked in the envy of my classmates, and was probably totally insufferable.

When I landed my first real part as the lead in an *After School Special*, my dad and mom quit their respective jobs in finance and teaching to become my full-time managers. I was six years old and suddenly the breadwinner in the family. An *After School Special* is great, but it doesn't buy much bread for very long.

Even if it did, no child should be the sole source of income for her family.

Or so my therapist tells me.

But I was. Which meant that every audition I went to, I now had to nail it. I had to own it, I had to earn it, because if I didn't, "we were all in deep shit," as my dad was fond of saying. So I'd smile and jazz-hand and be charming, and I'd land those parts.

But I never saw a dime of what I made.

My parents didn't defraud me. For a long time, I thought they had. I was a famous teenager getting by on a $100-a-week allowance in a $1,000-a-week town, and they were driving around in fancy cars and in limousines. My mom wrote a book—*Raising Amber*—and my dad started managing other starlets' money. They became masters of getting their own names in the press almost as often as mine.

When I started asking questions, my parents would always hush down my concerns. Did I want for anything? Didn't we live in a beautiful home? I should just keep up my end of the bargain and they'd keep up theirs. Why rock a boat that isn't sinking?

Like any teenager, I found them stifling. I was sure they didn't understand me and there were a lot of slammed doors. Connor was the one who suggested I wasn't like any teenager. I made the money, I had the power, and if I asked, the courts would give both to me. So I applied for a formal emancipation, and that's when I found out the truth.

My parents weren't stealing from me—they were living off their 20 percent "management" fee, which was all written down and legit—they had just made the bulk of what I earned inaccessible. It's called a trust, and it's all legit, but when you're sixteen and 80 percent of a lifetime of jazz hands is sitting in there, unreachable until you turn thirty, it feels like something's been stolen.

It was "for my own good" they told the judge. The trust was a stricter version of laws that were already in place, laws that were meant to prevent the very thing I'd been so sure was going on. I'd be protected against the possibility of what a child star might become, my dad said in his elegant, structured voice. I couldn't spend it all or snort it all or give it all away to some shyster who persuaded me to start my own record label. The judge seemed to be on my side. I mean, he gave me what I wanted—freedom—but he couldn't undo the trust, and so I was sixteen and free and broke and unprotected against what I could become.

And then I became that thing like it was my life's work.

But even after all of that, I was still ready, deep down, to forgive them. Especially when they finally started listening to my yelps for help and forced me into rehab. When we reconciled during the family counseling sessions we had at the Cloudspin Oasis, I was sincere.

I thought they were too.

Then I got out of rehab and I made a few stupid mistakes—staying out late, attending parties I should've stayed away from—and though I was still clean and sober, the press turned to vultures and my parents had a choice: believe me or believe what they read. They picked the latter, and somewhere in there they decided that the way to reach me, the only way to speak to me, was through the marvels of television.

So every couple of months since I left rehab, when I'd be worn down by some combination of bad press and Connor, they'd pop up on something like *Entertainment Tonight*, saying how worried they were about me, how they just wanted me to be well.

"We just want our daughter back," my mother would say, wearing her stoic face, and it would be up to me to try to convince the disbelieving world that they were the ones in the wrong. And because I didn't want to sink to their level, I had to somehow do that without telling the world they'd lost all their money on reckless spending and bad investments—exactly what they were so sure *I'd* do. That all they were after now was another piece of me.

"We just want our daughter back," my mother says to Cathy Keeler now, staring into the camera with a trembling lip.

It's all Amber Sheppard all the time over at Cathy Keeler these days.

"Of course you do. What parents wouldn't?"

"I hate my fucking parents," I say to Bernard, who's watching the show with me once again, and who's been bellyaching about his thirty years in the business going down the toilet since he got here.

"Great. Thanks. Like that's helping."

"At least you're not in the middle of some public intervention—"

I bring my hand to my mouth as a flash of an idea hits me.

"What?"

"I've either just had the best idea ever, or the worst. I'm not sure which."

✪

"I feel like we've been here before," Katie says.

We're sitting on her couch after I've finally convinced her to let me come over. She was as suspicious as I would've been, and now that I've laid out my plan, I can't tell what she's thinking.

"And that's exactly why you're going to help me, right?"

She grins. "Of course. I'm sure my editor will be delighted."

"Did you get in trouble after the press conference?"

"Are you kidding? That press conference was the highlight of his year. I'll probably get promoted."

"Happy to help."

"I'm not going to take it! Besides, when I told my sponsor about it, I thought she was going to have kittens. I'm in danger or 'regressing,' apparently."

"Tell me about it."

She looks concerned. "Are you okay on that front?"

"I'm okay. I've been going to a lot of meetings."

"So I've read."

"Katie, can I give you a bit of advice?"

"Of course."

"You need to stop believing everything you read. And you really need another job."

"I know. Especially since I'm about to hand in my resignation."

"Seriously?"

"Yeah. My sponsor's right."

"But working at *The Line* is your dream job."

"It is. But it keeps coming at this crazy price. I can't . . . I need to start living with integrity, if that makes any sense."

"I get it. But why didn't you say so before?"

"Because I just made up my mind to do it."

I laugh in spite of myself. "You're crazy, you know that?"

"So Henry's always reminding me."

"What are you going to do for work?"

"I'm sure something will turn up. Word on the street is I have some pretty awesome celebrity connections."

My face falls.

"Hey, I was just kidding. I'm going to try to get a job on talent alone and see where that takes me."

"That sounds like a good plan."

She hesitates. "I'm sorry we stopped speaking, you know."

"Why was that, anyway?"

"You tell me."

"I don't know . . . maybe once the trust is gone, it's hard to be friends for real."

"And here I thought it was because you didn't want people thinking we were a couple anymore."

I laugh. "Are you kidding? You were, like, my most stable girlfriend ever."

She wrinkles her nose. "Anyway, let me go call Bob while I'm still in his good books."

She leaves and I wander around her living room. I've never been to this apartment, the one she lives in with Henry. The space is nice, comfy, cozy, homey. She has a few framed photographs on the mantel. A selfie of her and Henry at a concert, both of them looking happier and more relaxed than when I knew them. Katie and her sister, her parents, Henry's. Most surprising of all, a shot of the four of us—Connor, Henry, Katie, and me—taken on one of our last days together in rehab, arms slung over each other's necks. Connor, looking droll and detached. Henry stealing a glance at Katie. Katie and I in the middle, laughing.

Ready to take on the world.

Or so we thought.

"That's the last picture I have of us together," Henry says, coming into the room. "Seems like a lifetime ago."

He's dressed to go out for a run.

"It feels like just yesterday to me," I say.

"That too."

"Thank you for what you said at the funeral."

"You already thanked me."

"I know, but I thought it was worth doing again."

"You're welcome."

"I don't think I've ever heard you say that many words at once before."

He gives me a half-smile. "You know me."

"I thought I did. I'd like to."

"That'd be good. I know Kate would like that too. She told me what you're doing."

"Is it totally crazy?"

He shrugs. "I hope it works."

"Me too."

"Olivia helping with it?"

My stomach falls.

"What is it?" Henry asks. "She wasn't at the funeral. You guys get in a fight?"

"I . . . there's something you should know."

I ask him if he can keep a secret, even from Katie, then tell him as simply as I can. That somehow Olivia and Connor had hooked up. That Olivia's apparently pregnant with Connor's child. That we aren't speaking. Henry just listens as I talk, shaking his head slightly as if there's a fly buzzing around it.

"Are you sure?" he asks when I'm done.

"Of course not. Part of me is still hoping it's some sick dream. That Connor didn't really sink that low."

"Well, I don't mean to speak ill of the dead, but I think you're going to have to face that very possibility. In a way, it doesn't surprise me."

"Really?"

"It's the ultimate final fuck-you, right? To both of us."

"From Olivia, or Connor?"

"Both of them, I suspect."

"Maybe I'll find out."

"How?"

"Because Olivia's an integral part of the plan."

Chapter 12

Good for Nothing

The day before our first big scene together, the one where TGND and Charlie (Connor's character's name) kiss for the first time, Connor showed up at my place. I was already totally crushing on him, and I was in full freak out mode about our upcoming scene together. I was still living with my parents, but they were gone for the weekend, trusting that our cook and housekeeper were enough to keep me out of trouble. Which they were, back then . . .

The doorbell rang and there he was standing on my front porch, looking adorable and sheepish and confident all at once.

"How do you know where I live?" I stammered out, my teeth chattering with a sudden chill.

"You're adorable, you know that?"

He came inside and plopped onto the living-room couch, making himself at home. He pulled the pages of his sides out of his back pocket and dropped them onto the coffee table.

"I thought we might rehearse," he said.

I sat down next to him. "Oh?"

"Mmm-hmm." He leaned in close.

"What's to rehearse?" I asked, trying to act casual, though my palms were sweaty. "It's only a kiss."

He leaned in even closer and I could feel his breath on my lips. "I don't know about you, but I'd prefer our first kiss to be just between you and me."

✪

With Katie working on her end, I decide to tackle the first item on my list, which is to go see Olivia. I need her on board before I can be sure my plan is going to work. Okay, nothing's going to make me sure of that, but I need to see her anyway.

Olivia lives a couple of miles away from me, and I'm not too worried about the press following me there, as there's nothing odd—to them—in me going to see her.

They think they know everything there is to know about me.

They don't know shit.

Not yet, anyway.

If Olivia's surprised to see me, she manages to hide it. She looks thin and terrible, and there's nothing pregnancy-glowy about her. There is, however, the barest hint of a bump pushing out her T-shirt, which I take in with a sick heart.

"So, it's true?" I ask, my eyes on her stomach.

"Yes."

"And you're keeping it?"

"Yes. I told Chris. He left."

I'm sorry, I think reflexively. But I'm not, so I don't say it.

"You must think I'm a terrible person," she says.

"I'm thinking all kinds of things."

"I didn't mean for it to happen."

"Why does everyone always say that?"

"Maybe because it's true."

"So how did it happen, then?"

She shakes her head, but I know she'll tell me. She loves gossip, even if it involves herself.

She makes us some tea, and we sit at her kitchen table. Eventually she starts speaking.

"He'd just left rehab, you know, when you and Danny got engaged. You weren't taking his calls—no one even knew he'd been in rehab—and he asked me to meet him. To talk. He sounded so sincere. You know how he can . . . could . . . be."

"I know."

"We met at a restaurant out of town. I had to drive for an hour to get there. He was keeping a low profile, he said. Trying to change his patterns. He was drinking soda water, and we ate really good homemade pasta, and we talked for the first time in like forever. We were friends too, you forget that, but all that time I was with Henry, we spent a lot of time together. You know how Connor didn't like to be alone."

"Uh-huh."

"We were always hanging out together when Henry was living in his pool house. And sometimes when we both couldn't sleep, we'd run into each other in the kitchen and we'd end up talking."

"Over milk and cookies?"

"Yeah, sort of."

"I can't believe what I'm hearing."

"What?"

"You slept with him back then too, didn't you?"

"No! I swear to you, Amber. I didn't. It was only that one time, one stupid time. And he was talking about you the whole night. It didn't have anything to do with me really."

"Except, you're the one who's pregnant."

"I know that, okay?"

"What were you thinking, though, honestly?"

She leans back and rests her hands on her stomach. An ache flows through me. Because even though I don't want a baby now, today, no way, I used to fantasize about having one, one day, with him. What the two of us together would produce. What silly name we'd choose.

"I wasn't, obviously," she says. "But when he stopped talking about you and we started talking about the past, the times when you weren't around, I don't know, something about it, his focus, was on me for once. It was … seductive. But I could also tell he really wanted a drink, so when he asked me to stay with him, I did."

Of course she did. Because, like Henry said at the funeral, no one said no to Connor when he asked you for something. He was like kryptonite to reason.

"Okay, enough. I've already heard too much."

"I'm sorry."

"Right. You said. Christ, your pregnancy news is going to be bigger than Kate Middleton's."

She blanches. "I know I don't have a right to ask, but will you promise not to tell anyone? Not right away. I need . . . I need this to be secret for a little while longer."

A spasm of pity flows through me, but I squash it.

Because I'm the one who needs her right now, and pity isn't going to get me what I want.

"Actually, what I need, Olivia, is for this *not* to be secret right now."

Chapter 13

I Love It When a Plan Comes Together

It takes two weeks to gather the necessary information and get the essential people to agree to be where I need them to be, when I need them to be.

It's a weird two weeks. In the moments when I'm frantically planning and plotting and going over the details with Katie, I can forget, almost, the whole reason I'm doing this. But when I stop moving, even for a minute, it hits me. Connor is dead, *dead*, he's never coming back. That's when everything stops, and I get lost in that thought.

I get lost.

And this makes me want to get really lost, bottom-of-a-bottle, end-of-a-line lost, so I'm attending as many meetings as I can, and I've got my sponsor on speed dial. In reality, the only thing that's saving me is the impossibility of me going anywhere where I could score something right now—unless someone else did it for me, which they won't.

Once a day, Bernard sends me a roundup of the craziest stories circulating out there.

The AA meetings you're attending are really a front for a group of addicts getting together to shoot up.

Now that Connor's gone, you're playing for the other team again and have reunited with your first girlfriend, Kate Sandford.

You really are pregnant [insert picture of me looking "healthy"], *and the baby is Connor's.*

Your parents are setting up another intervention for you, and they'll be filming it for a "very special episode" of that show, Intervention.

Mostly these stories make me laugh—which I assume is why Bernard's sending them to me, either that or he's worried they're true—and strengthen my resolve to go through with the plan. Sometimes, though, they send a shiver down my spine because they're hitting a little too close to home. Like a thousand monkeys sitting at a thousand typewriters: someday one of them is going to hit on the truth.

I just hope it's not before Thursday.

✪

"Are they all in there?" I ask Bernard, pacing in the hall outside the ballroom at the Ritz, where I had the disastrous press conference a month ago.

"Yup. Every single one."

"What did you have to say to get them here?"

"Depends on who we're talking about. But the word 'intervention' worked pretty well."

"It would."

He puts his hand on my shoulder. "You sure you're ready?"

"I've got to go through with it now, don't I?"

"Probably."

"Let's do it."

"Knock 'em dead in there."

I square my shoulders and enter the room, Bernard following close behind. Eleven people are sitting in a circle, like they used to do in group back in rehab: The four paparazzo I've identified as the most influential/rabidly interested in me. Olivia. My parents. Katie. Henry. My sponsor.

Sitting at the head of them all, ready to direct the proceedings, is my former therapist from rehab, Saundra.

Saundra's a short, plump, woman in her fifties who let her hair go its natural grey. She loves all-things-dog, as Katie would say, and often expresses that love through clothing. Today's no exception. She's wearing a hand-knitted sweater with the words "A House Is Not a Home without a Dog" stitched across her large breasts.

This is going to be awesome.

"Amber, hello," Saundra says in her best obey-me-or-face-the-consequences voice. "Glad you could join us. And dressed appropriately too."

I plaster a smile on my face. I used to make costumes in rehab from the craft supplies and wear them to group.

You know, for kicks.

"What's all this?" I ask in the little-girl-lost voice I perfected on

The Girl Next Door. "Is everyone here just for me?"

"Of course we are, dear," my mother says through her perfect teeth, her diction clipped. "It's an intervention. I believe you're familiar with them by now?"

A low shot, but I can take it. I have to.

I look around the room, making eye contact with each of this motley crew one by one. The paparazzi are fiddling with their phones, clearly taking pictures despite our rules. Katie's smoothing her hands over a pile of file folders sitting in her lap. Henry's smiling at me encouragingly. My parents seem annoyed that there's no one here to film this. (Okay, that's just my interpretation of their sour expressions, but I bet I'm right). My sponsor's impassive, not for the plan, but not against it either. Olivia's wearing a loose blouse and her face is paler than usual. I get to Saundra last, and she's giving me the look she gave me when she told me I could finally leave rehab.

Her words that day come back to me.

"You're strong, Amber. Remember that on the outside and you'll do fine."

I am strong.

I am strong.

I am strong.

"All right, folks," I say into the bated silence in my real voice. "Sorry to disappoint you, but this isn't an intervention. At least not for me. Shall we get started?"

✪

"So," I say now that I have their attention, pulling a letter out of my pocket. "You know how this works, right? I tell you how your actions have been affecting my life, and when we're done, you agree to stop what you've been doing and seek help."

"I'm not going to rehab," scoffs Paparazzo Mike from the press conference, his wife and partner in crime nodding her head vigorously next to him. "In fact, I'm not staying."

"Oh, I'd stay if I were you," Henry says, standing as if to block him from leaving. "Trust me."

A quiet guy, Henry, but you don't want to cross him.

Mike looks chastened but also ready to bolt at the first

opportunity. His wife's shooting daggers out of her eyes if that was, you know, actually possible.

"Don't worry," I say. "You're not going to have to go to real rehab, though some of you might need it, and if you do, I'd highly recommend the Cloudspin Oasis."

"For what?" asks that Johnson guy who was also at the press conference.

"We'll get to that," Saundra says. "But first I think you all owe the favor of your attention to Amber."

She nods at me and I start reading.

"Each of you is here because you've all had a part to play in what my life is like these days. Whether you believe it or not, I've been clean since I left rehab. I've been working really hard to show everyone that I'm okay, that I can be trusted, that I deserve a second chance. But you all have made that impossible. So I'm here today to ask you to stop.

"Mike, Johnson, et al. I know you think it's your job, but every time you follow me around, every time you take a picture that makes me look as if I'm in trouble, you're undoing what I'm working for. I get why you do it. I get that this is how you get paid, but don't you think you've made enough off of me? Isn't there something better you could be doing with your lives?

"I'm not saying you're responsible for Connor's death or anything, but he hated you guys and what you did to him, to me, to his friends. He hated it. It's not your fault he had a drug problem, or that the public buys the crap you sell, but you sure don't help. People believe what they read, especially where there's a photo that seems to confirm it. And, sometimes, when you know everyone's waiting for you to fail, it makes it easier to do so. You know you're kind of living up to expectations, and there's some comfort in that."

The paparazzi are squirming in their seats, looking uncomfortable but not convinced.

I turn to my parents. "Mom and Dad, I know you think you're trying to help me when you go on TV, but you're not. Because every time you do this, you're believing the worst of me. Instead of giving me the benefit of the doubt, you take whatever they throw out there as true. I know I've given you lots of reasons to believe them, and I know things haven't been good between us in a long time, but you could've tried asking me first. Just once.

"To be completely honest, lots of the time, I think I hate you. But I don't want to hate you. If you took the time to know me again, you'd see that most days I'm doing all right. I'd do a lot better if I had your silent support."

I steal a glance at my parents. My mom's crying and my dad's lip is quivering.

Am I a terrible person if this gives me some satisfaction?

Maybe this will be enough to convince them, at least.

Then again, maybe not.

"Olivia. I know you're sorry, but you really hurt me. I'm not sure I'm ever going to be able to trust you again, which makes me so sad because it's hard to imagine my life without you in it. But there's a toxic part of us together, clearly. Why else would you have . . . done what you—" I stop as a sob escapes her. A lump starts to form in my throat and I don't think I can go through with it. I can't throw Olivia under the bus simply to get myself out from under it.

I make a decision. Come what may.

"Your agreeing to be here today means a lot. I've been thinking about it, and about what happened. That'll be between us, okay? You don't have to worry."

Olivia slumps down in her seat, the air let out of the balloon of her worry. I feel relieved that I don't have to be the bad guy. I just hope the plan still works.

I turn back to the paparazzi. "I don't expect you guys to believe what I say. Why would you? Why would anyone? That's why Sue's here. She's my sponsor. Has been for a long time. I've authorized her to confirm I'm clean. That I've passed every drug test she's ever given me, including the one I took this morning."

Sue nods.

"How do we know she's who you says she is?" Johnson asks.

"Because I say so," answers Saundra with as much authority as someone in a dog sweater can muster.

"Me too," says Henry.

"Me three," says Katie.

"Me four," says Olivia. "And everyone knows that Rule Number Five of Being a Super Famous Person is: Don't lie about your drug status when you're trying to win over your enemies."

I'd laugh at that one if it wasn't for my dad saying, "Me five."

Now it's my lip that's quivering.

"Me fucking six," says Bernard.

"Yeah, well, so, even if that's true," says Mike, "why should we do what you want?"

"Because you're good people, really deep down?" I say hopefully.

"This is my job. I have a mortgage to pay. Mouths to feed."

"So you're not going to stop?"

The paparazzi are silent.

I sigh. "I thought that might be your answer so . . . after the carrot comes the stick." I turn to my parents. "You remember how this works, right? If you won't do what I ask willingly, there have to be consequences. I don't want to have to do this, but if you don't stop, I'm cutting you off."

My mother looks taken aback. "We're doing fine without you, dear."

"Uh, well, no you aren't. Right, Dad?"

My dad looks at his hands. "Yes, well, dear, um, we took quite a hit in the last stock market crash and . . . Amber's been topping up our account every month."

"Why didn't you tell me?" my mother asks.

"I . . ."

"I asked him to keep it quiet," I say, because what the hell—one more lie in my lifetime won't hurt.

My dad looks up at me, and for the first time in a long time I see what I've been looking for. Pride.

My mother surprises me too. "Thank you, Amber. That's very generous of you."

"You're welcome. Do we have a deal?"

"Of course. Even without the money. You only had to ask. You're our daughter."

Would it really have been that simple? All these years? So easy to say now, and impossible to confirm.

"That . . . that means a lot. Okay. Now, for the rest of you . . . Take it away, Katie."

Katie looks nervous but assured as she addresses the paparazzi. "I've got a folder here with each of your names on it. Inside is just a taste of what it's like to be on the other end of your cameras. Shall we begin with you, Johnson?"

She flips open the top folder. "Oh, yes. You sure hang out in a lot of parks. At night. I wonder what your wife would think about that?"

"But, but, but . . . that's blackmail!"

"Is it really?" I say. "Taking pictures of people when they're in public places and publishing their bad deeds for all to see is a crime, is it?"

"You just threatened me, and I've got it on tape." He holds up his phone, waving it back and forth while it flashes that it's "recording." "I wonder how much I could sell this for?"

"I'm pregnant with Connor's baby!" Olivia says.

"You're what?" Katie asks.

"I'm pregnant with Connor Parks' baby," Olivia says again, then buries her face in her hands, sobbing.

Henry scans the shocked faces. "You all get that?"

Chapter 14

Wish Fulfillment

In my perfect world, this is what happens.

1. The paparazzi see the error of their ways—or are terrified enough of what's in Katie's folders—that they stop. Stop following me around, living outside my apartment building, going through my garbage, shouting my name.

2. Those paparazzi who aren't persuaded to stop—who I have no dirt on—follow the lead of group one and come to the realization that there are other fish to fry. That there are melting icebergs flooding the oceans to photograph, or baby seals to save, or whatever. #anythingbutme.

3. Those who don't fall into groups one and two are so consumed by the Oh-my-God-Olivia-Amber's-best-friend-is-pregnant-with-Connor's-baby news that they give me the breathing room I'm looking for.

4. My parents decide to take a vacation at an ashram in India where there's no TV, no Internet, no cell phone signals, and where they learn to be serene and generous and self-aware. Oh, and also: headstands. Because headstands are awesome and Zen.

5. In all the free time I've gained not avoiding the paparazzi, I get a life, and meet with directors, and read scripts, and convince the stupid perfume company that my life really is fabulous and they shouldn't cancel my contract. I find the perfect project and get cast in it, and I'm proud of the job I do in it, no matter what anyone else thinks.

6. Oh, and I totally learn how to do a headstand too. And in my new Zen-blood-rushing-to-my-head state I learn to accept Connor for what he was, and to remember the good, and jettison the bad. My heart is open enough to find someone else to love, the right person at the right time who loves me the way I deserve to be loved.

If I could control the world, that's what would happen. But since I do not, this is what actually happens.

1. While the paparazzi I brought to my intervention seem to have gone on "vacation," they were immediately replaced with four who looked just like them. They've bred like cockroaches, only they don't skitter away in the light of day.

2. The Vacationing Paparazzi materialize in Europe, where they start to terrorize royals and leather-skinned socialites.

3. The Replacement Paparazzi, and the general public, are totally consumed by oh-my-God-she's-carrying-Connor's-baby-etc. Olivia—her life is holy hell right now—but that doesn't mean they're leaving me alone. Hell, no. The *Am-ber. Am-ber. Am-ber* chorus is so loud that the police actually intervene for once and I had a day, *a day* of silence. I got a fucking day.

4. My parents . . . well, they haven't gone to India, but they're staying quiet for now. Except for the press conference they gave to talk about how "disappointed" they were in Olivia, who they'd treated as a second daughter, though they were there for her if she needed anything for the baby. Which they repeated on Cathy Keeler, and *Entertainment Tonight*, and . . . you get the picture. At least they aren't talking about me. But they totally should've listened to me about the headstand thing.

5. Danny won't take my phone calls, or return my texts, or answer my emails. I just want to tell him I'm sorry for the way I treated him, but he clearly doesn't want to hear it. He

is, however, dating one of Connor's ex-girlfriends, so I'm guessing that he's not over it.

6. The perfume company cancels my contract. As Bernard tells me, they have a warehouse full of my perfume and he hopes "I like the fucking smell," because I'll be wearing it for the rest of my fabulous life. I know this is probably ironic, or good metaphor material, but mostly it just stinks.

7. The only offer I receive is to star in some *Fifty Shades of Grey* knock-off. I actually spend five minutes considering it. A low moment.

8. Cathy Keeler invites me on the show to tell "my side of the story." Since I'm pretty sure "my side of the story" will be met with snarkiness and potentially a "surprise" appearance by my parents, I decline.

9. I get sideswiped by the Connor-is-dead-thing on a regular basis. I'll be okay for a bit, going through my closet, getting rid of clutter, and then *wham!*—some memory hits me upside the head and almost knocks me out cold.

10. I do not find my Zen place.

11. I cannot do a headstand.

But, *but*, while I don't control the world, I do still live in fantasyland, so there's no telling what can happen next.

Chapter 15

I Saw Your Picture Today

Well, of course, there *is* telling what happened next.

So . . . two weeks later.

I'm driving.

I'm driving Connor's car, and Olivia's sitting next to me. We're on the road to Connor's parents' house.

Right. I should probably unpack that a little.

Connor's car. It was still where I left it two months ago when I drove it home after jumping out of Connor's airplane. I sent Bernard to find it. He came back full of his usual profanities. The car was covered in tickets and had one of those yellow boots attached to its tire and did I know how many "fucking phone calls" it took to get something like that taken care of when it wasn't your own car?

I hugged him. "You're the best, Bernard."

He looked a bit surprised. "Oh, yeah, well, happy to do it. Only..."

"Why do I want the car?"

"Sure."

"I have a few ghosts to get rid of."

What I don't tell Bernard is that I really want the car to *visit* a ghost. Because Connor's smell still lingers in this car. Lemon and spice and something I could never put my finger on. Scattered in the trash on the floor, between the seats, are clues to how he spent his last days. And, I don't know, but some stupid part of me is hoping that there's a . . . message or something for me in there. Something Connor left behind which would explain why he was texting me in those months before he died, what he was doing with me all those years, how he actually felt.

Some sort of closure.

I know it sounds stupid.

I know it sounds like I think I live in one of the movies I wish I was still starring in.

But here's the thing.

After I spend an hour in my building's garage with a flashlight going over every inch of the car and collecting all the bits of his life into a trash bag, I sit in the driver's seat, my hands on the wheel, staring at the concrete wall in front of me. At some point I start to cry at the continued unfairness and stupidity of it all. Connor took so many risks with his life, and yet what ended it was a mechanical failure that could've happened to anyone.

What are you supposed to make of that?

How are you supposed to process that?

How am I . . .

Oh God, I miss him, I *miss* him. Even though I'd gotten used to him no longer being in my life, I knew he was still out there in the world. In an instant, I could Google him and see what he looked like yesterday. I could read his stupid tweets—*Hanging with my dudes! Digging this!*—or scroll through the photos he'd post sporadically on Instagram, or pick up a magazine and read the latest speculation about his love life.

Yes, I did all these things.

I don't want to think how often.

But now, there's nothing new. Nothing to feed my desire for information. Oh, people are still posting old photos of him, old stories, old montages, but there's nothing *new*. Except the one big thing. Something, someone, that will never belong to me.

But the baby is coming, he or she is coming, and that's why I pull myself together. I drive through the parking lot with Connor's baseball hat on my head, hoping that the *Am-ber*-chanting crowd will be disoriented enough by the unfamiliar car, this stupid early hour, or the fact that I'm even leaving the building to notice me quickly enough to follow.

As the garage door creeps up, the rising sun hits me in the eyes. I lower the visor to block it, and that's when I find what I was looking for.

Something that was wedged into the visor's flap floats down and lands in my lap.

A picture.

A picture of me and him.

A picture of us.

✪

The picture takes away my whole time advantage with the paparazzi, but I don't care. I hold it with my fingertips, careful not to crease it any further. Of course I have photos of us together, there are thousands of them, but this one was Connor's. How long has it been up there, in the visor, tucked away from view? Connor's had this car forever, he never throws anything away, but I didn't know he had this.

It's such an ordinary photo. One we'd taken the first time we moved in together, when I was eighteen. We had some silly notion that we'd be "regular folks" and packed his stuff into a U-Haul and hauled it, well, ourselves. We're wearing grubby clothes. He has a streak of dirt across his cheek. We both look tired but satisfied. I can't remember which one of us pulled out our phone to take it. Each of us has an arm extended, holding the phone steady. Our other arms are around one another, the sides of our faces mashed together.

He moved out three months later, and back in again three months after that. And so on. But this was the first time. This was when I still thought it was going to work out. Forever. Against the odds. That our love would bind us through the chaos.

Maybe it's not true, but it feels like this picture holds the last time I felt hope.

✪

When I finally snap out of my reverie, I tuck the photo back into its place for safekeeping. That's when I realize the car is surrounded by a group of grubby men staring at me, their cameras at the ready, a million shots already probably taken. I touch the gas pedal and edge the car forward, and eventually they fear enough for the safety of their feet to get out of my way.

I drive to Olivia's slowly. They're following me anyway, so there's no need to put anyone's life at risk. When I get to her house,

I pull over quickly and bolt for the front door. Olivia opens it as if she's been expecting me, and I tumble through and close it as the street fills up behind me.

"What are you doing here?" she asks.

"Twenty questions?" I say, and she smiles.

Chapter 16

Three Minutes Past the Hour

This is how it ends.

The drive to Connor's parents' house takes four hours, which we pass mostly in silence.

When we finally get there, I want Olivia to go in alone, but she's too scared, so I take her hand and we walk up the front steps together. Our unwanted entourage is parking right and left. The curtains on Connor's house tweak to the side, revealing Connor's mom, Charlene. She looks scared. Our eyes meet and she shakes her head. *How could you?* she's asking me.

I didn't, I want to scream, but screaming's not going to help anything right now.

Might feel good, though.

Instead, I concentrate on walking up the steps, counting on the fact that their not letting us in would cause a bigger scene than doing so.

I'm right. Connor's dad opens the door in time with my knock, and we're inside Connor's childhood home, sitting next to each other on the couch he used to jump on when his mother wasn't looking like we're two teenagers about to disclose an unwanted pregnancy. Which is, I guess, fitting.

"What do you want?" Charlene asks. She's pale and gaunt and sad and angry. About what you'd expect.

"I thought you should meet Olivia."

"We've met."

"Right, but not, you know, properly."

She turns to Connor's dad. "I can't. Please, Don—"

"—No, Charlene. I think she's right. If Olivia's really carrying our grandchild . . . You are carrying our grandchild, aren't you?"

"Yes," Olivia says softly.

"Are you sure?" Charlene asks.

"Of course she's sure," I say. "Do you think she'd be going

through all of this if she wasn't sure?"

"I didn't mean anything by it. I . . . Connor moved in a fast crowd."

He did. Only, Connor was the one with his foot on the accelerator. But I can't tell her that.

"You're going to be grandparents," I say instead. "Congratulations."

Don and Charlene exchange glances, as if they're trying to decide if this is good news or bad. But in a world full of terrible news, this is good.

It's good.

It's good.

It is.

❂

An hour later, Olivia and I get up to leave, with promises—on Olivia's part—to visit again soon. When we get to the door, Olivia dashes off to pee, and Charlene and I are left alone together for the first time in . . . I can't even think of the last time we were alone together.

"I'm really sorry," I find myself saying.

"For what part?" she asks.

This is hopeless.

"For . . . for whatever it is you think I'm responsible for. I was only trying to love him. I love him."

She gives me a hard stare. For a minute I think that on this day of bygones, she might see her way to finally letting go of whatever it is that's been keeping me on the outside.

But no.

"We shouldn't hurt the ones we love," she says.

"I know. I didn't mean to. And he . . ."

"What?"

"Nothing."

I reach down my shirt and pull out the necklace. My heart on a string. A family heirloom, he said when he gave it to me. Because you're my family now.

"Do you . . . do you want this back?"

She glances down and her eyes fill with tears. "Do you want to give it back?"

"Of course not. But if it would . . . if it would help, then maybe . . ."

"He wanted you to have it. I don't know why, but he did, so."

Because he loved me, he loved me, he did.

"Okay . . . I . . . thank you." I clutch the necklace, feeling the heart warm in my hand, like there's a small beat inside it. As if there's something pumping blood and oxygen and life into this lifeless metal.

"I will take his baseball hat, though," she says, her eyes travelling to my head.

I reach up to touch it. "This?"

"It's his, isn't it?"

"Yes, but . . ."

She smiles sadly. "It was a joke, Amber. You keep it."

I don't know how to react to his mother cracking jokes. I don't want to cry in front of her.

"Oh. I . . ." I reach into my pocket. "I have Connor's car. I mean, it's outside. Here are the keys." I hand them to her. "You should have it."

"You don't want that too?"

Moment over, I guess.

"I . . . what? No. I don't want . . . I don't want anything. I never wanted . . ."

"Let's just leave it at that, why don't we?"

"Okay, Mrs. Parks."

She nods and turns away, the keys clutched in her hand in the same way I'm holding onto her platinum heart. Maybe she thinks if she holds on tight enough it will bring Connor back, or keep our memories of him intact. I've thought that.

I'll give the hat to his son or daughter, I realize. His child with Olivia. When they're the right age to appreciate it. When they're old enough to know something about their dad, and how much they would have meant to him. Old enough to not rip this hat to shreds. If it's a boy, maybe when he loves a girl, a million days from now, I'll give him this heart too, to give to her. When he's sure she's the right one, even if Olivia isn't. Even if the world thinks otherwise.

Until then, I'll keep it.

I'll keep them both safe for the child he will never meet.

✪

Olivia and I grab a lift back to the city with one of the paparazzi, a new one who's intimidated enough to keep his questions to himself. Another four hours of near silence later, we drop Olivia off first. He looks like he wants to ditch me too, but I don't make any move to get out of the car, and eventually he drives me to my place. Even though he's new at his job, he knows exactly where it is.

Before I climb out of the car, I take a piece of paper from my purse and scribble something on it.

"This is my cell number," I tell him.

He blushes. Man, he needs to toughen up.

"Look, I don't expect—"

"—Don't be an idiot. It's my way of saying thanks. If you're really in a bind, for a photograph or whatever, call me and I'll give you something. A one-time offer. But if you give it to someone else, I'll know it's you."

He smiles nervously. "Thank you."

"Thanks for the lift."

I get out of the car. As I ride up the elevator to my apartment I start to feel lighter than I have in a long time. It's late afternoon, and the lowering sun is streaming in through the curtains. I stand at the window and pull them back. The paparazzi are still below, but in my imagination, there are less of them. Or maybe not. Maybe they'll always be there, and that's just life. My life.

And I don't know, but standing there in the sun, I guess I have one of those moments of clarity people are always talking about in AA. Maybe it's the sunshine. Maybe it's the fact that I came away from Connor's parents' house with my heart still intact.

My platinum heart, anyway.

But this is what I'm feeling like.

I'm feeling like I can see the end of Connor. Not his real end, of course. That already happened. The end of him and me. Not all those fake endings we had over and over. Not our real ending that we had on the plane. Not a perfect ending, but maybe, *maybe*, an ending I can live with eventually.

I loved him. He loved me. Nothing's ever going to change that. But it changed me, it changed me so much that I lost myself. I floated out into the ether until I wasn't visible to myself anymore.

But I'm back on earth now, and I think it's finally a place I can stand to be. It's a place where I can make a life for myself.

I don't know why it took him dying to see that. I can't think it's a blessing. But that doesn't mean I can't make something good of it. I can be smart enough, finally, to learn from someone else's mistakes.

Only time will tell. I'm lucky enough to have it.

Back when we met, it felt like my whole life was full of time, that we'd have enough time to do everything together.

But what I remember most was how nervous I was when I met him, how I stayed nervous every time I was around him. I flubbed my lines in our first couple of scenes and got a talking to from the director. A stern phone call was placed to my parents. Even before anything happened between us, he already had the ability to spin my life out of control.

Because that's how I felt with him—*spun*.

Maybe I should've paid attention to that, but instead . . .

We were standing on the kitchen set of *TGND*, in between takes. The scene called for us to make a cake for a mutual friend's birthday. We had to frost the cake, and he was supposed to get the frosting somewhere cute, the end of my nose or my forehead, I can't remember, and say something like, "You've got something there . . ." and . . . you get the picture.

"You've got something right . . . there," Connor said, reaching towards my cheek and sweeping a dollop of frosting from it. As he brought his finger to his mouth he double-raised his eyebrows, flirting, suggestive, and a shiver ran through me.

The director called "cut," and I watched as he sucked his finger, thoughtfully, then tipped his arm to look at his watch.

"It's three minutes after," he said.

"It's . . . what?"

"Three minutes after the hour." He leaned forward to talk directly into my ear so the boom and body mics wouldn't pick up what he was about to say. So only I could hear him.

"That's the first time I touched you," he said. "But it won't be the last."

And now . . .

The sun lowers another notch and hits me in the eye. My phone buzzes in my pocket and I reach for it reflexively. A text from Bernard, which I can read later.

The numbers on the phone's clock say it's three minutes past the hour, and this is what I will remember forever.

Three minutes past the hour.

That's our time.

Amber's Playlist

Chapter 1: "Dirt and Dead Ends"—Indigo Girls

Chapter 2: "Falling Apart"—Matt Nathanson

Chapter 3: "Afterlife"—Arcade Fire

Chapter 4: "Let's Stop Calling It Love"—Mozella

Chapter 5: "Fade Into You"—*Nashville* cast, featuring Sam
Palladio and Clare Bowen

Chapter 6: "New Slang"—The Shins

Chapter 7: "Flightless Bird, American Mouth"—Iron & Wine

Chapter 8: "Goodbye My Lover"—James Blunt

Chapter 9: "All Over Now"—Eric Hutchinson

Chapter 10: "Speak for Me"—John Mayer

Chapter 11: "History Repeating"—Propellerheads

Chapter 12: "Look Where We Are Now"—Teddy Geiger

Chapter 13: "Save Me"—JJ Heller

Chapter 14: "Wishin' and Hopin'"—Dusty Springfield

Chapter 15: "Picture"—Kid Rock, featuring Sheryl Crow

Chapter 16: "Little Cosmic Girl"—Brett Dennen

Keep Reading for an Excerpt from
Catherine's Latest Novel, **HIDDEN**
Available Now

Prologue

Jeff

The last thing I had to do that day was fire Art Davies.

I hate firing people. Truly. Of all the things I hate about my job—and their number are legion—having to tell someone they can't come to work anymore is the worst.

But the consultants had been called in (again), and the recommendation was right there on page 94 of their 217-page PowerPoint presentation: *The accounting department is overstaffed by 1.2 people.*

1.2 people!

Who talks like that?

When I got the summary of the consultants' report—there's a guy in Reports whose entire job is, you guessed it, summarizing reports—I flipped to the page he'd so helpfully marked with one of those yellow stickies with a red pointing finger on it and my heart sank. Next to the recommendation that I reduce my department by 1.2 people were the words: *Art Davies??*

Art Davies?? I read again, and my heart fell a little further. Because those question marks might've seemed innocent, but they were as uncertain as a bullet to the chest.

Report Summarizing Guy is the direct liaison between management and the consultants. His job is to implement enough of their suggestions to justify the consultants' ridiculous fees, and enable management to make their own PowerPoint presentation for the board claiming that 74 per cent of the recommendations had been implemented.

So job well done.

Art Davies. *Fuck.* Art Davies is the guy who hired me six years ago, back when the department was a third the size and there weren't any consultants around to notice that he wasn't really the guy you wanted to entrust hiring and firing to. Truth be told, Art wasn't the guy you wanted to entrust a lot of things to, but he was a great guy. Always in a good mood, quick to forgive your failings, always sending around some hilarious YouTube video right when your day was at the nadir of sucking.

I'd worked hard to help him escape the last two rounds of consultants. But he'd Peter-Principled himself to the head of the department, as guys like Art are wont to do, and when I'd been at the company enough years to satisfy the brass, we switched jobs. A couple years ago, I went up and he went down, and Art, good ole Art, took it so well you almost could've believed he didn't give a shit.

"Couldn't have happened to a better person," he said, slapping me on the back like we were in some sitcom. "Look forward to working for you."

I'd gone home in a deep funk and told my wife I wanted to quit. It took her hours to talk me out of it. Phrases like *great opportunity* and *think what we can do with the extra money* bounced off me, my resolve untouchable.

Until she said, "Art will probably be happier this way, you know. He never struck me as someone who wanted responsibility."

I didn't want to admit it, but she was right. Art probably would be happier if he didn't have to hire and fire people, or report to the board, or implement Report Summarizing Guy's suggestions.

I didn't quit. Instead, I traded desks with Art, putting the silver-framed picture of my family in the faint dust outline the picture of his family had left, and went back to work. And now it had come to this.

And I couldn't help wondering, if rising to the level of your own incompetence has a name, does having to fire the guy who hired you have one too?

When I'd phoned Tish to tell her about it, she'd made a small noise of sympathy. She knew how much I hated firing people.

"Why don't you let HR do it?" she asked.

"No, I can't do that."

"Why not? Management does it all the time. Trust me."

"Aren't you always calling them pussies when they do?"

She laughed, a melodious thing. "Yeah, yeah. I wouldn't call *you* that though."

"Sure."

"You know I wouldn't."

I sighed. "Okay, maybe not. But still."

"You have to do it."

"I have to do it."

"Let me know if you want some tips."

"You mean if I want your five-point plan for firing people effectively?"

"How the—" She clucked her tongue. "You little bastard. You read the whole report, didn't you? Unbelievable."

I smiled, even though she couldn't see it. "I like having all the information."

"Uh-huh."

"I have to keep ahead of those guys. You never know when they're going to train their high beams on you."

"You are so *busted.*"

"I should get back to work."

"Have fun with your numbers!"

"You know I will!"

I hung up and ran my hand over my face. As much as I liked talking to Tish, it didn't change the fact that Art had to go, and I had to do it.

I spent Friday doing everything I could to put off the inevitable. But there wasn't anything I could do about Art's termination package, which was sitting on my desk. A blue, folded packet full of helpful hints about what he might do with his future, and a single sheet of paper outlining his *non-negotiable* severance package. Fifty-six years old, twenty-two years with the company, not in management—thanks to me—meant he was getting 28.4 weeks of severance pay.

What was it with this company?

Couldn't they ever think in round numbers?

But no, they couldn't, because that would affect the pie chart, and that might end up with an eventual recommendation that they be *terminated*??

So at four forty-five I gave one last sigh, and checked my email one last time. There was a message from Tish saying simply: *Good luck.*

Thanks, I typed back, *I'll give you the blow-by-blow later.*

I hit Send, turned off my computer, put my hands on my desk and pushed myself up.

Inertia's a funny thing; even though it doesn't make any sense scientifically speaking, I swear I had to push harder than usual. My steps down the hall also seemed heavier, thicker, like the feeling you get in a dream when you're trying to run. Treacle air, molasses legs.

Art was sitting at his desk, an Excel spreadsheet open before him. He was squinting at the screen over the rim of his glasses. He never did get those bifocals his ophthalmologist had recommended a few months ago, and as per the package tucked under my arm, he had four weeks to do so or he was shit out of luck.

He glanced up at me. "Hey, Jeff, you think you could help me out on this one? I can't seem to get the columns to balance." He shook his head, half mocking, half puzzled.

"Why don't you leave it, Art?"

"I have to get it done today. It's on my goal sheet."

"It's okay. You don't have to do it."

"You're a braver man than—" He stopped abruptly as he caught sight of the folder. "That's not . . . I mean . . . they couldn't . . . not after all this time . . ."

"Why don't we go into the conference room?"

He rose to follow me, shocked into silence. If my footfalls seemed heavy before, my feet were cement blocks now. We made it into the conference room, and Art slumped into the nearest chair. I tried not to slump into the one across from him. *Project an air of confident compassion,* Tish had counselled me. But what did that mean, really? I had compassion all right, but confidence?

There was no way I was ever going to be able to look Art in the eye again.

Concentrate on outlining the details of the package. She'd said that too.

I opened the packet in front of me and read the text from the one sheet in a monotone. *"We're sorry to inform you that your position has been eliminated. In appreciation for your years of faithful service to the company, we're happy to offer you—"*

I stopped reading because Art was crying. Not sobbing, just a stream of tears flowing from behind his glasses and collecting on his shirt in spreading pools of wet.

Christ. What was I supposed to do now?

Sometimes a reassuring hand on the shoulder is appropriate. Tish's words kept coming. *Sometimes I let them cry, just being there for them.*

I opted for the latter, partly because I couldn't bring myself to move my hand, but also because it seemed like that kind of gesture should come with words, and I had no idea what to say. That it was all going to be okay? That he'd find something else, something better? That he wasn't going to lose his house, or have to raid his kids' college funds to avoid it? I couldn't say any of those things. It wasn't going to be okay, and he wasn't going to find something else.

Guys like Art never do.

Not at fifty-six.

Not when the guy firing you is the guy you hired.

I have to hand it to Art, though. Sixty seconds of silence was all it took him to pull himself together.

He lowered his glasses and wiped his eyes with the back of his hand. "I expect you have to finish reading that."

"Yes. I'm sorry. It's—"

"—Company policy."

"I'm sorry," I said again.

"It's okay, Jeff. Don't give it another thought."

I hung my head. Art was comforting me for firing him. And for a moment, it actually made me feel better. Was I the worst person ever?

"This will be over soon," I managed to get out.

"Thank you."

After I read through the rest of the miserly conditions of his package, Art had to suffer the final indignity of having me watch while he packed up his stuff. Back when I started here, a guy in Art's situation would've been given a proper send-off. They'd have called it "early retirement," and there would've been a nice lunch, maybe even a nice watch. Art would've gotten slightly drunk, and someone would've made a speech about how much Art had done for the company, told a funny story or two about his time here, and said he would be missed.

But that was a long time ago. Now, I pulled white, flat-packed bankers' boxes from the supply closet, folding them together mechanically, wondering how many were required to pack away twenty plus years.

It turned out to be two.

When it came right down to it, Art travelled light.

He finished packing. I pulled a dolly out of the same closet and stacked his boxes on it over his protests that he was perfectly capable of doing it himself.

"I know you are, I said. "I want to do it, okay?"

"You're the boss."

He smiled sheepishly, a silent acknowledgment that none of this would be happening if I wasn't the boss. Or maybe it would. If I'd quit when I wanted to, someone else would've been promoted, or brought in from the outside, and they might not have protected Art from this day as long as I did. Who knows?

Either way, I still felt like an asshole.

Art picked up his light tan coat and slipped his arms into it. By tacit agreement, we left the building by the fire exit, which kept us from having to do the I'm-being-escorted-from-the-building walk past the still half-full office.

I followed him, wheeling the squeaky dolly behind me, hoping his boxes didn't tip over. I'd done my best to look away while he was hastily emptying his desk, remembering a story he was fond of telling about the first person he had to fire. Don Somebody, who was an old-school, three-martini-lunch guy whose lack of productivity in the afternoons had finally reached the notice of the higher-ups without any help from consultants. Art had tried to track the guy down before lunch, but he kept getting pulled into meetings.

He finally caught up with Don around three. He was standing next to a filing cabinet like the leaning tower of Pisa, and he didn't take the news well. After his swearing had been reduced to short, sporadic bursts, he'd agreed to clear out his desk. Don reached for the top drawer, but it was stuck. Art wasn't sure if Don was so drunk he forgot what was in the drawer or if he simply didn't give a shit, but he lifted his foot off the ground and placed it on the desk for leverage, tugging on the drawer's handle for all it was worth. It came unstuck, and Don and the drawer tumbled backwards as a stack of porno magazines fanned across the floor.

The way Art tells it, Don was completely unfazed. He collected up his magazines and held them against his chest.

"Only thing I wanted to take with me, anyway," he said as he lurched out the front door.

I took the wheelchair ramp down its long, gently slopped diversion from the front doors. Art waited for me at the bottom, his face now expressionless, his posture screaming *Let this be over.* I followed him through the parking lot, past rows of cars backed carefully into their spots. He stopped in front of a silver Pontiac Vibe. The left side mirror was cracked.

"Kids," Art said. "You know how it is."

"Sure," I said, though, thankfully, Seth wasn't old enough to drive yet.

He popped the hatchback and I stacked his boxes inside, closing the lid with a *thud.* We stood there awkwardly for a moment; was this a handshake occasion, or were we going to hug it out? Art solved my dilemma by reaching out his hand.

I took it. "You take care of yourself," I said. "Sorry about all of this."

"I'll be all right. Who knows, I might take up golf."

"Call me if you do."

He folded himself into his car. The engine started neatly and Art was composed enough to look left, then right, then left again before exiting his spot. I watched him drive slowly through the lot, towards the sun's setting orb, shielding my eyes against its glare. I'm not sure why, but I felt responsible for him while he was still on company property. Once he made it off the lot, I felt, he'd be all right.

After his car was absorbed into the end-of-day traffic, I turned back towards the building. The sun was glinting off the large windows, and I couldn't face going back inside. I decided, instead, to walk home. The air was warm, my car would survive the weekend where it was, and I had my phone. I could file my report on Art's firing on Monday.

I tucked my hands into my pockets and took a shortcut through the parking lot to the main road. Home was a mile away, and the sun felt warm on my face. I closed my eyes for a moment to concentrate on the feeling of it, and I guess that's why I never saw it coming.

Chapter 1

Late for Dinner

Claire

Friday's an ordinary day at the daycare, if there is such a thing when you have thirty children between the ages of one and four under your supervision. There are no visits to the emergency room, despite the fact that Carrie Myers gets a penny stuck in her nose. The parents make their usual number of calls, from zero, in the case of the Zen 20 per cent, to ten, in the case of Mandy Holden.

It's all because of the video cameras. Standard issue in daycares these days: twelve cameras (six in the baby room, six in the toddler room), all strategically positioned so any concerned parent can watch their child all day long via computer if they want to.

I'm glad Seth graduated prior to the invention of the Daycare Cam. I tell myself I'd be in the Zen 20 per cent, but I have enough evidence to the contrary to know I would've had the camera feed open on my computer screen eight hours a day.

But since that was never a possibility, I can let myself feel annoyed when I catch a scuffle out of the corner of my eye on a toddler room monitor (they're arrayed around my desk like I'm the head of security, which, I suppose, I am), and I hear LT's wail through the wall moments later. I count down the seconds. Three, two . . .

"Hi, Mandy," I say as I pick up the phone, not bothering to pretend I don't know who's calling. Mandy Holden calls between five and ten times a day with questions ranging from her son's, LT's, caloric intake to any incident she picks up on from the black-and-white video she watches all day long. (LT is named after his father, Trevor, because he's "Little Trevor" in looks, expression, everything. Around here, when the parents aren't listening, he's referred to by the name he's earned: "Little Terror.")

"Did you see that, Claire? That other kid—"

"—His name is Kyle."

"Whatever. He pushed LT over! He needs a serious time out, and if you're not going to talk to his parents, I will."

"You know I can't call a child's parents every time there's an isolated incident."

"Isolated incident! He did the same thing last week."

"Actually, if you'll recall, it was LT who pushed Kyle that day. Kyle pushed back in retaliation."

"Retaliation my ass. I saw the whole thing."

"I'm sorry, Mandy, but I reviewed the video as per your request. LT was definitely the aggressor." In fact, at this very moment, LT's meting out his revenge on Sophie Taylor by stealing her snack. I'm sure I'll be getting a call about that too.

"Are you suggesting my son has anger-management issues?"

"Of course not. I'm simply saying that three-year-olds, particularly three-year-old boys, often get in scuffles. You can't read too much into it, no matter who the instigator is." I glance fondly at the picture of Seth at that age pinned above the monitors. He's smiling with a little-teeth grin, a perfect mixture of mischief and innocence.

"Instigator!"

"It's only a turn of phrase." I pause deliberately and lower my voice. "However, if you'd feel more comfortable removing LT from our care, you're perfectly entitled to do so."

I'm playing my trump card. Every daycare in town is full to the max. Mandy isn't going to give up her slot unless LT's taken out of here on a stretcher.

"I never said anything about taking LT out of Playthings," she huffs.

"Well, I seem to be getting a lot of these calls lately, and we do have an extensive waiting list."

I can hear her grinding her teeth. "I'm expressing *concern* for my *child*, Claire. I don't think that deserves a threat."

"Now, now, calm down. You know we all love LT. We don't want him to leave. I want you to be happy."

"I'm happy," she says. "LT is happy."

"That's great. So we don't have an issue?"

"No. Everything's fine. I have to get to a meeting . . ."

"Talk to you soon."

We hang up and I rest my head in my hands. I love running Playthings, I really do, but sometimes, particularly on the days when the Mandys of the world are in high gear, I wish I were back in the grown-up world, dealing with grown-up problems.

Of course, that world was full of adults complaining about the way their babies were being treated too.

Much to the chagrin of some of the parents, my lunch hour's a sacred thing. I don't accept calls—in fact, I can't be reached at all, and unless you're a fellow student at the music conservatory, it's like I don't exist.

This is a rule I implemented soon after I started Playthings, when I was still being swept by the waves of sadness connected to why I chucked my law career and started the daycare in the first place.

"You need to make time for something purely yours," my doctor told me when I complained about having trouble sleeping, and the general listlessness I still felt. "Something that brings you joy. Did you have anything in your life like that? Before?"

I could've taken the easy road and told him that what I used to do was run frantically between work and child care, that I hadn't had time for anything else. I hadn't had much time for me. Instead I said "Piano" in a small voice, even though I hadn't played in years. I no longer even owned a piano; we'd left it behind when we bought the house because it wasn't worth paying the extra money the movers wanted for something I touched only to wipe away the thin layer of dust that marred its glossy surface. It felt like an easy decision then, but now I wasn't so sure it was the right one.

"Piano it is," Dr. Mayer replied in a voice that brooked no opposition. And something about it, something about how it was connected to me *before*, caught hold in my brain.

I left his office and drove to the conservatory, which was located a few minutes away. I parked my car and looked through the windshield at the brightly painted building. Like Playthings, it was clearly a place for kids. I could see the child-painted mural inside made up of bass clefs and off-proportion guitars, a relic from my own childhood, many hours of which were spent in that very building. They gave adult lessons too, they always had, but the whole thing screamed Suzuki Method, and I almost didn't go in.

But I'd said I would, and so I did.

In a few minutes, I had a lesson scheduled for the next day with Connie. The receptionist met my tentative request for Mr. Samuels, the kind teacher from my youth, with a blank stare.

Connie turned out to be a taciturn Germanic blonde who had somehow ended up in Springfield. ("How?" I asked early on. "Complicated," she replied in a clipped tone that invited no further questions. "We work on scales today.") When she realized that I knew more than basic chord structures, she started giving me more and more complicated pieces. And once my muscle/brain memory kicked in, I started to make something of them.

I kind of hated Connie in those early days (I suspect the feeling was mutual). I complained to Jeff one night, a few lessons in, that Connie had missed her calling as a drill sergeant.

"So quit," he said as he stripped down to his underwear and climbed under the covers.

"What do you mean?"

"If you're not having fun, fuck it."

I slipped in beside him, resting my back against the headboard. I flexed my fingers. They were full of a dull ache, like the early onset of arthritis.

"I kind of feel like it'll be fun eventually. Or maybe that's the wrong word." I paused, not knowing how to talk about looking for joy, and how it sometimes felt like it was only a few notes away.

"Well, she can't be the only game in town, right?"

It turned out he was right, but the two younger teachers I tried were so used to the kids-who-were-working-just-hard-enough-to-appease-their-parents that they'd grown soft, their fingers slow. When I sight-read the pieces they'd put in front of me, saying "Now, this should be a real challenge," they'd get these funny looks on their faces, like *that wasn't supposed to happen*. One of them told me bluntly: "You should be playing with Connie." The other simply "forgot" our lesson one day and never called me to reschedule. Either way, I got the message.

So back I went and here I am, sitting on the hard piano bench in a room with perfect acoustics playing Debussy's *Reverie*. Connie's standing next to me, waiting to turn the page. My left foot's working the soft pedal, my right heel's keeping time. As the haunting melody tumbles out I lean in, like I'm trying to catch the notes, gather them close. And now there's *un poco crescendo* and the music's flowing through my fingers, into my chest, suffusing my brain. The world is receding, receding, and yet I feel, for lack of a better word, alive.

When I get home around five, Seth's at the dining room table pretending to do his homework. But our in-need-of-replacement TV is still emitting that strange, staticky sound it does for the minute or so after it's been turned off, so I can tell what he's really been up to. What I need to decide is whether I'm going to call him on it.

Letting Seth be home alone for the hour or so between when the bus drops him off and when Jeff or I get home is a new thing we're trying since he turned twelve in February. He lobbied hard for the freedom, showing us that he was old enough, responsible. He kept his room clean, his grades went up, and he actually put down his PS-whatever-they've-gotten-to-now when we asked him to. We agreed to it on a trial basis until the end of the school year. If he doesn't screw up, we'll talk about making the arrangement permanent.

It's nice to have the extra money, though I miss the chats Ashley (Seth's long-term after-school babysitter) and I used to have at the end of the day. The updates she'd give me about how Seth acted when Jeff and I weren't around. As Seth gets older, the opportunities to observe him when he isn't aware of it are few and far between. Teacher-parent interviews, reports from his grandparents, my chats with Ashley, that's about it. Now, if I want to know what my son really thinks, I'll have to resort to spying.

Seth raises his head slowly and gives me the smile that melts my heart every time I see it. I've steeled myself against it to a certain extent (I had to), but it's worked on babysitters and women in grocery stores his whole life.

"Hey, Mom."

"Hey, buddy, how was school today?"

"Same."

"You have a lot of homework?"

"The usual. I'll be done soon."

"It needs to be done before dinner," I say in a tone that's way too close to my mother's.

"Mom, jeez, it's Friday."

I raise my hands in surrender and head to the kitchen, thinking about what's in the fridge, wondering whether I should cook or if we should go out for dinner. Jeff mentioned something last night about having to fire someone today, someone he was upset about. Did that mean he'd rather go out or stay in? Out is a distraction; in might mean him drinking too much and brooding about it.

Out it is, then.

I pick up the cordless phone and dial his work number. When he doesn't answer, I try his cell. It rings and rings and then goes to voicemail. I glance at the clock. It's five fifteen, about the time he usually gets home on Fridays. Maybe his meeting went long; firings are never easy. And it's such a nice day out, he might've decided to go to the driving range and hit a few balls first. He doesn't like bringing bad work energy home if there's a way he can leave it behind.

I spend the next hour working on a new piece Connie's given me (Haydn's Sonata in F Minor), working out the fingering, letting the notes linger in my brain as I tap them out silently on the kitchen table, and now it's a quarter after six and Jeff really is late. Another round of calls to his cell and work phone get the same result as before, so I dig my cell out of my purse and text him: *Home soon?* I hold the phone in my hands, waiting for his reply, but none comes. Eventually, it powers down, like it's tired of waiting.

I feel a small trace of annoyance, but I brush it away. He often gets lost in whatever he's doing. His focus is something that astounds me still after all this time. Getting mad about it would mean I was mad at something fundamental about him, which I'm not.

But I *am* hungry. "Seth, do you want to order in?"

Seth comes bounding into the kitchen like an eager dog, lunging for the drawer where we keep the takeout menus. After a small skirmish, we decide on pizza, Seth promising that he'll eat at least one slice of vegetarian so he gets some vegetables today.

Jeff still isn't home by the time the pizza arrives, so I don't bother setting the table. We eat at the kitchen table while I gently probe Seth about his week. He dodges my questions like he always does, his mouth full of food, his answers a combination of "Jeez, Mom, honestly," "Dunno," and "All right, I guess."

I try not to take it personally. I try to remember how I was at that age, the secrets I kept.

I let Seth take his last piece of pizza into the living room while he finishes his homework. I bring our dishes to the sink, which sits in front of a window overlooking our front lawn. I'm washing the dinner plates when I notice that it's almost seven thirty, and now maybe I am mad that Jeff hasn't even bothered to check in.

A police cruiser slows to a stop in front of our house. There are two uniformed officers in the car. The one I know, whose name I can't bring to mind though we went to high school together, is sitting behind the wheel. He's gripping it like he's girding himself to do something unpleasant. I watch them, curious, as they slowly exit the car, two burly men. I wonder if the neighbor's teenage daughter is in trouble again, but it isn't their walkway they're lumbering up; it's mine. My mind jumps to Seth. What could he possibly have done that's worthy of police attention?

Then my heart clenches with the sudden knowledge of why they must be here. My hands sit in the sudsy water, turning gently to prunes.

They're at the front door, and still I can't move. They don't look my way, just straight ahead, and push the bell, harder than they should. The chiming gong bounds through the house, a brassy sound I've never liked.

All this happens in real time, not slowed down or speeded up, only the time it takes for them to walk to the front door and ring my bell, but it's enough time.

"Mom!" Seth yells. "You going to get that?"

My brain is screaming *Go to the door! Don't let Seth be the one who answers it!*, but I can't bring myself to move. In this, of all moments, I can't bring myself to protect my son.

"Really," I hear him mutter as he clicks off the TV and shuffles towards the front door.

Now my feet are moving, my mouth is open, but I can't get the words out. I don't beat Seth to the door, which is swinging open, revealing the officers. And my son, my beautiful, intelligent son, sees the unpleasant task in their faces, turns towards me with a look of horror, and runs.

Haven't read SPIN?

Keep Reading for an Excerpt

Chapter 1

Must Love Music

This is how I lose my dream job.

It's the day before my thirtieth birthday when I get the call from *The Line*, only the most prestigious music magazine in the world, maybe the universe. OK, maybe *Rolling Stone* is number one, but *The Line* is definitely second.

I've wanted to write for *The Line* for as long as I can remember. It still blows me away that people get paid to work there since I'd pay good money just to be allowed to sit in on a story meeting. Hell, I'd sit in on a recycling committee meeting if it'd get me in the front door.

So, it's no surprise that I almost fall off my chair when I see their ad in the Help Wanted section one lazy Sunday morning. I sprint to my computer and wait impatiently for my dial-up to connect. (Yes, I still have dial-up. It's all this struggling writer can afford.) When the scratchy whine silences, I call up their webpage and click on the "Work for Us!" tab, as I have too many unsuccessful times before, and there it is. A job, a real job!

The Line *seeks self-motivated writer for staff position. Must love music more than money because this job pays jack, brother! Send your CV and music lover credentials to kevin@theline.com.*

I spend the next twenty-four hours agonizing over the "music lover credentials" portion of my application. How am I supposed to narrow down my musical influences to the three lines provided? Then again, how am I going to get a job writing about music if I can't even list my favorite bands?

In the end I let iTunes pick for me. If I've listened to a song 946 times (which, incidentally, is the number of times I've apparently played KT Tunstall's "Black Horse and the Cherry Tree"), I must really like it, right? Not a perfect system, but better than the over-thought-out lists sitting balled up in my wastepaper basket.

And it works. A few days later I receive an email with a written interview attached. I have forty-eight hours to complete the questionnaire and submit it. If I pass, I'll get a real, in-person interview on *The Line*'s premises! Just the thought of it has me doing a happy dance all over my living room.

Thankfully, the questionnaire is a breeze. *Pick five Dylan songs and explain why they're great. Pick five Oasis songs and explain why they suck. What do you think the defining sounds of this decade will be? Go see a band you've never seen before and write five hundred words about it. Buy a CD from the country section and listen to it five times. Write five hundred words on how it made you feel.*

I stay up all night chain-smoking cigarettes and working my way through two of my roommate Joanne's bottles of red wine. She's always buying wine (as an "investment," she says), but she never drinks any of it. What a waste!

When the sun comes up, I read through what I've written, and if I do say so myself, it's a thing of beauty. There isn't a question I stutter over, an opinion I don't have. I've even written it in *The Line*'s signature style.

I've been waiting for this opportunity forever, and I'm not going to fuck it up.

At least, not yet.

The next two weeks are agony. My brain is spinning with negative thoughts. Maybe I don't really know anything about music? Maybe they don't want someone who can merely parrot their signature style? Maybe they're looking for some new style, and I'm not it? Maybe they should call me before I lose my goddamn mind!

When the spinning becomes overwhelming, I try to distract myself. I clean our tiny apartment. I invent three new ramen noodle soup recipes. I see a few bands and write reviews for the local papers I freelance for. I clean out my closet, sort all my mail, and return phone calls I've been putting off for months. I even write a thank-you letter to my ninety-year-old grandmother for the birthday check she sent me on my sister's birthday.

I spend the rest of the time alternating between obsessively reading *The Line*'s website (including six years of back issues I've read countless times before) and watching a young star's life explode all over the tabloids.

Amber Sheppard, better known as "The Girl Next Door" (or "TGND" for short), after the character she played from ages fourteen to eighteen on the situation comedy called—wait for it — *The Girl Next Door*, is Hollywood's latest It Girl. When her show was cancelled, she starred in two successful teen horror flicks, followed by a serious, Oscar-nominated performance for her turn as Catherine Morland in *Northanger Abbey*. She's been working non-stop since, and has four movies scheduled to premier in the next five months.

When she wrapped the fourth film just after her twenty-third birthday, she announced she was taking a well-deserved, undisclosed period of time off to relax and regroup.

And that's when the shit hit the fan.

Anyone really seeking relaxation would rent a cabin in the woods and drop out of sight. But not TGND. She partied all night, slept all day, and dropped twenty pounds from one photograph to the next. There were rumors appearing on such reliable sources as people.com, *TMZ*, and *Perez Hilton* that she's into some serious drugs. There were other rumors, of the Enquiring kind, that her family had staged an intervention and packed her off to rehab. It seems like there's a new story, a new outrageous photograph, a new website devoted to her every move every day, and I read them all.

Such is the fuel that keeps my idling brain from going crazy as I wait and wait.

The call from *The Line* finally comes the day before my birthday at 8:55 in the morning.

Mornings are never good for me, and this morning my fatigue is compounded by the combination of another bottle of Joanne's investment wine, and the riveting all-night television generated by TGND's escape from rehab. (Turns out *The Enquirer* was right.) She lasted two days before peeling off in her white Ford hybrid SUV, and the paparazzi who follow her every move captured it from a hundred angles. It was O.J. all over again (sans, you know, the whole murdering your ex-wife thing), and the footage played in an endless loop on CNN, etc., for hours. I'd finally tired of it around three. The phone shatters my REM sleep what feels like seconds later.

"Mmmph?"

"Is this Kate Sandford?"

"Mmm."

"This is Elizabeth from *The Line* calling? We wanted to set up an interview?" Her voice rises at the end of each sentence, turning it into a question.

I sit bolt upright, my heart in my throat. "You do?"

"Are you available at nine tomorrow?"

Tomorrow. My birthday. Damn straight I'm available.

"Yes. Yes, I'm available."

"Great. So, come to our offices at nine and ask for me? Elizabeth?"

"That's great. Perfect. I'll see you then."

I throw back the covers, spring from bed, and break into my happy dance.

This is the best birthday present ever!

I'm going to nail this! After years and years of writing for whoever would have me, I'm going to finally get to write for a real magazine! For *the* magazine. Yes, yes, yes!

"Katie, what the hell are you doing?" Joanne is standing in the doorway looking pissed. Her curly orange hair forms a halo around her pale face. She looks like Little Orphan Annie, all grown up. Her robe is even that red-trimmed-with-white combination that Annie always wears.

"Celebrating?"

"Do you know what time it is?"

I check the clock by my bedside. "Nine?"

"That's right. And what time do I start work today?"

I know this is a trick question.

"You don't?"

"That's right, it's my day off. So why, pray tell, are you dancing around and whooping like you're at a jamboree?"

Despite the inquisition, my heart gives a happy beat. "Because I just got the most fabulous job interview in the world."

Joanne isn't diverted by my obvious happiness. "I think the answer you were looking for is, 'Because I'm an inconsiderate roommate who doesn't care about anyone but herself.'"

"Joanne ..."

"Just keep it down." She turns on her heel and storms away.

As I watch her leave, I wonder for the hundredth time why I'm still living with her. (I answered her in-search-of-a-roommate ad on

Craiglist three years ago, and we've had a love/hate relationship ever since.) Of course, she's clean, pays her share of the rent on time and never wakes me up when I'm trying to sleep in because she's yelping with joy.

Then again, I've never seen Joanne yelp with joy …

Ohmygod! I have an interview at *The Line*!

I resume my whooping dance with the sound off.

I spend the rest of the day vacillating between extreme nervousness and supreme confidence. In between emotional fluctuations, I agonize over what I should wear to the interview. I lay the options out on my bed:

1. Black standard business suit that my mother gave me for my college graduation. She thought I'd have all kinds of job interviews to wear it to. Sorry, Mom.

2. Skinny jeans, kick-ass boots, T-shirt from an edgy, obscure nineties band, black corduroy blazer.

3. Black clingy skirt and grey faux-cashmere sweater with funky jewelry.

I settle on option three, hoping it strikes the right balance between professional and what I think the atmosphere at *The Line* will be: hip, serious, but not too serious.

In the late afternoon, I receive a text from my second best friend, Greer.

U free 2nite?
No. Very important blah, blah am.
Must celebrate bday.
Bday 2morrow.
Aware. Exam in 2 days. Party 2nite.
No.
Insisting.
Must sleep. Need beauty for blah, blah.
Never be pretty enough to rely on looks for

blah, blah. Still insisting.
LOL. Need new friend. Still can't.
Expecting u @ F. @ 8. Won't take no for answer.
No.
LOL. 1 drink.
It never ends with 1.
Will 2nite, promise.
Can't.
I'm $$.
Well … maybe just 1.
Excellent. CU @ 8.

I throw down the phone with a smile, and try to decide whether any of my outfits will do for a night out with my college-aged friends.

I'm a nearly-thirty-year-old with college-aged friends because the only way I've been able to survive since I graduated from college (and the bank stopped loaning me money) is to keep living like I did when I was a student, right down to scamming as much free food and alcohol as possible on the college wine-and-cheese circuit. I met Greer this way two groups of friends ago. She's the only one who stuck post-graduation. She thinks I'm a fellow graduate student who writes music articles on the side to pay for my education and that tomorrow's my twenty-fifth birthday.

My own-age friends have all moved to nicer parts of the City. They work in law firms and investment banks, have dark circles under their eyes, and pale skin. Their annual salaries are twice what it cost me to educate myself, and the only wine and cheeses they go to are the cocktail parties given by their firms to woo new clients.

They mostly don't approve of the way I live, the part they know about anyway, but I mostly don't care. Because I'm doing it. I'm living my childhood dream of being a music writer. It's not a well-paying life, but it's the life I've chosen. On most days, I'm happy.

If I get this job at *The Line*, I'll be over the freaking moon.

Shortly after eight, I meet Greer at our favorite pub in my number two outfit: skinny jeans tucked into burgundy boots, obscure-band T-shirt, and black corduroy blazer to keep the spring night at bay.

The pub has an Irish-bar-out-of-a-box feel to it (hunter green wallpaper, dark oak bar, mirrored Guinness signs behind it, a whiff of stale lager), but we like its laid-back atmosphere, cheap pints, and occasional Irish rugby team.

Greer is sitting on her usual stool flirting with the bartender. The Black Eyed Peas song, "I Got a Feeling" is playing on the sound system. Greer orders me a beer and a whiskey shot as I sit down next to her.

"Hey, you promised one drink."

"A shot's not a drink. It's just a wee introduction to drinking."

Greer is from Scotland. She has long auburn hair, green eyes, porcelain skin, and an accent that drives men wild.

Sometimes I hate her.

Tonight she's wearing a soft sweater the color of new grass that exactly matches her eyes and a broken-in pair of jeans that fits her tall, slim frame perfectly. I'm glad I took the time to blow out my chestnut colored hair and put on the one shade of mascara that makes my eyes look sky blue. Nobody wants to be outshone at their almost-thirtieth-birthday party.

She clinks her shot against mine. "Happy birthday, lass. Drink up."

I really shouldn't, but … what the hell? Tomorrow is my birthday.

I drink the shot, and take a few long gulps of my beer to chase it down.

"Thanks, Greer."

"Welcome. So, tell me about this very important interview. Is it for a post-doc position?"

A post-doc position? Oh, right, that bad job you get after your PhD. Biggest downside to the fake-student personality? Keeping track of my two lives.

"Nope … Actually, I'm thinking of going in another direction. It's a job writing for a music magazine."

"Well, well, the bairn's growing up."

Greer is always tossing out colloquial Scottish expressions like "bairn" (meaning child), "steamin" (meaning drunk), and her ultimate insult, "don't be a scrounger" (meaning buy me a drink, you miserly bastard). Depending on the number of drinks she's consumed, it's sometimes impossible to understand her without translation.

"Had to happen sometime."

The bartender, Steve, brings us two more shots that Greer pays for with a smile. He only charges her for about a quarter of what she drinks, but since I'm often the beneficiary of his generosity, who's complaining?

She pushes one of the shots towards me.

"No, I can't."

"A wee dram won't hurt you."

"There's no way anyone actually says 'wee dram' anymore. That's just for the tourists, right?"

"I canna' break the code of honor of my country. And I mean 'honour' spelled the right way, with a 'u'. Now drink up, lass, before I drink it for you."

I upend the shot and nearly choke on it when Scott claps me hard on the back. He's a history major I met about a year ago at, you guessed it, a wine and cheese. We bonded while arguing over who had deeper knowledge of U2 and the Counting Crows (me, and me). His athletic body, sandy hair, and frank face are easy on the eyes, and given our mutual single status, I'm not quite sure why we've never hooked up. Maybe it's the fact that he's twenty-two, which puts him on the outside edge of my half-plus-seven rule. $((30 \div 2) + 7 = 22$. A good rule to live by to avoid age-inappropriate romantic entanglements.)

Scott orders another round. When it comes, he slides shot number three my way. I protest, but he flashes his blue eyes and wide smile, and talks me into it. Into that, and the next one. When Rob and Toni arrive a little while later, they buy the next two. And when those are gone, the room gets fuzzy and I lose count of the drinks that come next.

The rest of the night passes in a flash of images: Rob and Scott singing lewd rugby songs. Toni telling me she had a pregnancy scare the week before. Me blabbing on about how I'm going to nail my interview tomorrow, just nail it! Greer *Coyote Ugly*-ing it on the bar as Steve plies her with more shots. Someone dropping me off at my door, ringing the doorbell, and running away giggling. Joanne looking disappointed and resigned, then putting a blanket over me.

I lie on our living room couch with the room spinning around me, happy I have so many good friends, and an awesome job waiting for me to take it.

Tomorrow, tomorrow, tomorrow. I bring my watch to my face so I can see the glow-in-the-dark numbers. 3:40 a.m. I guess it's today. Hey, it's my birthday. *Happy birthday to me, happy birthday to me, happy birthday, happy birthday, happy birthday to me.*

"Katie!"

Someone is shaking me violently.

"Katie! Get up!"

The shaking gets more violent.

"Get orf me!"

"Katie, you have to get up. Now!"

Joanne rips the blanket off my face, and my eyes are flooded with light.

"What the hell's wrong with you?"

"Katie, pay attention. You have an interview in fifteen minutes!"

The world sinks slowly into my still drunk brain.

I. Have. An. Interview. In. Fifteen. Minutes.

Oh my God. *The Line.* The perfect job. The interview I have to nail. The interview I have in fifteen minutes.

I bolt out of bed and lurch towards the bathroom. The face that greets me in the mirror is a mess. My hair's sticking out at all angles, and my eyes are ringed with last night's mascara and eye shadow. I'm not completely sure, but I might also be a little green.

I take several deep breaths and command myself to pull it together. Under Joanne's reproachful eye, I fly into a fury of preparation, washing my face vigorously while simultaneously brushing the aftertaste of last night out of my mouth. After a few strokes of my hairbrush, I whip my hair back into a loose twist and pick up the clothes still laid out on my unslept in bed.

"What happened to you last night?" Joanne asks.

I slip into my skirt and pull the sweater over my head. "Nothing."

"Yeah, that's obvious."

"Thanks for waking me up."

"You know, someday, I'm not going to be around to take care of you."

"Joanne …"

"You'd better get out of here."

I take a last look at myself in the mirror (not so bad, considering) and run down to the street, searching desperately for a cab. I'd meant to take the subway to save money, but that plan's clearly out the window.

In a bit of good luck, a cab shudders to a stop the first time I fling my hand in the air. As it jerks and stops its way downtown, I fight a bout of nausea and nervously watch the minutes tick by on the clock.

8:56. 8:57. 8:58. 8:59.

Please, please, please.

9:00.

Shit, shit, shit.

9:01.

Breathe. Nope, can't breathe.

9:02.

Oh, thank God.

I throw money at the cab driver and sprint across the street through the rush-hour traffic. Cars screech and horns blare, but I somehow make it across alive. In the glass-and-marble lobby, I blank on the floor I'm supposed to go to. I wait through 9:03 and 9:04 at the information counter before I'm at the front of the line. Twenty-ninth floor, thanks! The elevator finally arrives at 9:05. 9:06 and 9:07 are spent stopping at what seems like every single floor between the lobby and the twenty-ninth floor.

I hurry out of the elevator, fling open *The Line*'s glass door, and try to walk calmly to the receptionist's desk. She has spiky purple hair and a ring through her nose. She can't be more than nineteen.

"Are you Kate?"

"Yes."

"Oh good, you're finally here."

It's then that I notice the clock on the wall behind her.

9:15.

I'm so screwed.

"I was stuck in traffic," I say weakly. Even to me it sounds like I said, "The dog ate my homework."

"Yes, traffic *can* be bad at this time of day."

"Yes."

"They're waiting for you in the Nashville Skyline room. It's down that hall."

"Thanks."

I walk down a long hall decorated with framed blow-ups of *The Line*'s past covers, passing a row of conference rooms. Abbey Road. Pet Sounds. Nevermind. Nashville Skyline.

OK. Here we go.

I check my reflection in the glass that frames an iconic shot of Dylan holding his guitar to his chest while he smiles down at the camera. Not quite the impression I wanted to make, but surely I'm not that color.

I knock on the door.

"Come in."

I take a deep breath and walk in. There are six men and women seated around one end of a long oak slab. Another photo of Dylan singing close-to-the-mike-harmony with Joan Baez dominates the wall behind them.

I smile nervously. "Hi, I'm Kate Sandford. I'm sorry I'm late."

A small woman in her early twenties with short mousy brown hair rises to greet me. She's wearing a tight black sweater dress that emphasizes her ample curves.

"Hi, Kate. I'm Elizabeth. We spoke on the phone? Why don't you have a seat?"

I sit at the end of the table and face the group. I'm having trouble focusing on their faces.

"Thank you so much for seeing me. I'm sorry about being late. Traffic."

"We understand? This is Kevin, Bob, Cora, Elliott, and Laetitia? Got it? Great? Let's begin?"

"Sure."

"Kate, we've been reading your pieces, and we really like them," says a man in his early thirties who I think is named Bob. Or maybe it's Elliott.

"Thank you, Bob."

"It's Kevin."

"Sorry about that."

"No problem. Why do you want to work at *The Line*?"

I clear my throat. "Well, obviously, it's always been a dream of mine. Of course, it would be. Anyway, I love music, and I've read

The Line forever, and, I don't know, do you believe in soulmates? Well, I've always kind of thought of this magazine as being my journalistic soulmate."

My heart starts to pound. What the hell is wrong with me? Soulmates? I actually used the word "soulmates" in an interview?

I scan their faces nervously. Cora (or is it Laetitia?) looks like she's trying to keep herself from laughing.

"What do you think you could bring to the magazine? What do you have that's different from everyone else out there?" Elizabeth's lilting voice brings back the nausea I suppressed in the cab.

Let's try this again. With feeling.

"Well ... I have this real pure love of music, you know? Like on my application? I had a lot of trouble narrowing down my musical influences because I really love all kinds of music. Like, I might dig a Britney Spears song, and the next minute be listening to, you know, Korn."

Did I just say I liked Britney Spears' music?

Cora/Laetitia isn't even bothering to cover up her laughter now, and I can't blame her. Elizabeth's way of speaking seems to be catching, and I'm becoming less articulate by the minute. I feel like I'm about to throw up.

"Talk to me about the bands you've been reviewing lately. Who stands out?" asks an older man whose name I can't even begin to guess at.

"Well, I really like this little neighborhood band called ... um ... hold on ... it'll come to me in a minute ..." The color creeps up my face as I draw a complete blank. "Um ... I'm sure I'll remember their name in a second ... Anyway, they're this great mix of ... you know, that band that's always on the radio now ..."

Total panic. I've known and remembered more about music than most teenage boys, and I can't remember the name of one of the biggest bands of that very moment. One of their songs was even playing on the radio in the cab on the way here.

I'm completely done for.

"Kate? Are you all right?" Elizabeth asks.

"I feel a little dizzy. Could I excuse myself for a minute to use the bathroom?"

Bob or Kevin, or whoever he is, frowns, but Elizabeth tells me where it is, and says they'll be waiting for me.

I walk quickly past Pet Sounds and Nevermind to the bathroom. The sharp odor of disinfectant catches in my nostrils. I splash water on my face, and grip the side of the sink as the room spins around me.

This cannot be happening! Please, please, please. Not today, not today, not today.

My stomach lurches, and I bolt into one of the stalls and throw up.

And up.

And up.

When I'm done, I slump to the floor and press my aching head against the cold tile wall, wishing I could disappear. The best day of my life has turned into the worst in an instant. I can't believe the interview I've waited half a lifetime for is coming to this.

"Kate? Are you in here?"

Elizabeth. Fantastic. Please, please, let a hole in the ground open up and swallow me. Maybe it can take me right down to hell, where I belong.

"I'll be out in a minute."

I struggle to stand, and the room begins to spin again. I lurch over the bowl and empty the remainder of my stomach's contents.

Elizabeth raps on the door. "Kate. What's going on in there? Kate?"

"I just feel a little sick …"

I throw up again, and this time what comes out doesn't resemble anything I've ever had to eat or drink and leaves a rancid, metallic taste in my mouth.

"You're drunk, right?"

"What? No! I just ate something bad. I think it was sushi."

"I can smell it on you? The alcohol?"

As her words sink in, I slide back to the floor in horror, my legs too weak to hold me.

"Maybe this is none of my business? But I've seen this before? There are good places, you know? Like for people with problems with alcohol?"

"I'll be out in a minute, OK?"

"I could give you a name? Like of a group? You know, AA?"

"I just need a minute," I whisper. "Just a minute."

"I don't think there's any point in continuing with the interview? When you're ready you can show yourself out?"

I listen to her leaving the bathroom, immobilized.

I know I have to get out of here, but I don't have the strength.

This is the worst, worst day of my life.

My thirtieth birthday is the worst day of my life.

Chapter 2

Redemption Song

When I finally pick myself up off the floor, I slink out of the building and somehow make it back to my apartment and my bed.

And that's where I stay for the next two days. I don't answer my phone. I ignore all texts. The only email I open is the formal "Thanks, but no thanks" I receive from *The Line*.

When I can't stand to be in bed anymore, I move to the living room couch and watch television twenty out of every twenty-four hours in a depressed wine haze.

There's a lot to watch. After the escape-from-rehab-high-speed-chase fiasco, TGND disappeared. The speculation is that she's holed up somewhere with her on-again, off-again boyfriend, Connor Parks, an actor eight years her senior.

Connor's career exploded when he made the first *Young James Bond* movie four years ago, and he now makes ten million dollars a picture. He's living like it, too, having apparently rented (some sources say bought) an island in the South Pacific, and this is where the press speculates endlessly that TGND is hiding.

"How can you watch that shit all day?" Joanne asks in her twenty-seven-going-on-forty voice when she finds me in a nest of blankets on the couch for the fifth morning running.

I kick an empty wine bottle under the couch. "What do you care?"

"I don't. But it might be nice to be able to watch my own TV once in a while."

Ah, crap. Who knew Joanne had feelings?

"I'm sorry, Joanne. I don't mean to be such a bitch."

She gives me a thin smile. "Apology accepted on one condition."

"What?"

"You take a shower, get dressed, and go outside."

"That sounds like a lot of conditions."

"Do we have a deal?"

"Deal."

And because Joanne is right, I take a shower and go outside for the first time in a week. The air is clean and mild in the way it only is in spring. The first buds are on the trees, and everyone on the street is smiling, or at least it seems that way.

For the first time in a week, I'm smiling too. It's hard to wallow in self-pity with warm sunlight on your face and the scent of cherry blossoms in the air.

I walk through my neighborhood, thinking about the state I'm in. Where my life is going. How I've been chasing a dream for eight long years without really getting anywhere. Something has to give, and I have a feeling I know what it is.

So, when I got back to the apartment, I call my best friend, Rory. We come from the same small town a few hours north and have been friends since kindergarten.

I fill her in on why she hasn't heard from me in so long.

"And then she said I should go to rehab, can you believe it?"

"Um, what time did you want to meet?"

Rory's an investment banker on the verge of a major promotion. We meet for lunch in her office building—the only place I know where she won't cancel on me at the last minute. There's this fifties-style diner in a corner of the lobby, and I wait for her nervously at the chrome counter.

"Katie!"

"Rory!"

I give her a quick hug, being careful not to wrinkle her navy banker's suit. Her olive skin rarely needs any makeup, but today she looks pale and drawn. She's even thinner than usual, and her cobalt blue eyes have circles under them that make her look more heroin-chic than City bigwig.

"Don't they ever let you outside?"

She makes a face. "I'll go outside when I make director."

"You could at least go to a tanning booth. Or, they have these moisturizers now that have self-tanner in them. They look pretty realistic."

"You're one to talk. Haven't you just spent the last week holed up in your apartment?"

"True enough."

The waitress takes our orders, and we catch up on the small

details of our lives.

"So, why'd you want to meet, anyway?" Rory asks as she picks at the plate of food in front of her.

"I need an excuse to see my best friend?"

"I thought that other girl, Greer, was your best friend."

"Don't be silly. She's just someone to party with."

"If you say so."

"Rory, you know you're irreplaceable, even if you become a big, snooty director-person who never has time for her friends."

Her eyes narrow. "*If* I become?"

"I meant when, of course."

"I hope so. Anyway, don't worry. I'll still have time for you."

"And I promise not to mind if you're too embarrassed to tell people what I do for a living."

"What do you do for a living?"

I start ripping my napkin into tiny little squares. "Yeah, well, that's kind of what I wanted to talk to you about."

"What's up?"

"I was, um, hoping you could get me a job. I'd be willing to do anything, like start in the mailroom or be your secretary. Whatever it takes."

She looks surprised. "You want to work at the bank?"

"Sure, why not?"

"But what about becoming a writer?"

Ouch. I thought I was a writer. Unsuccessful maybe, but still …

"I'm sick of eating ramen noodles," I say, trying to laugh it off.

"You can do some awesome things with ramen noodles."

"Yeah, I should write a cookbook or something. So, what do you say?"

She takes a small bite from her sandwich, thinking it over. "You sure you want to do this?"

"Yes."

"OK, let me see what I can do."

"You're the best, Rory."

"Don't you forget it."

"Like you'd ever let me."

Two weeks later, after more interviews than it should take to become president of a bank, I'm officially hired as the second assistant to the head of the Mergers and Acquisitions department.

I'm assigned a small interior office next to assistant number one and told I'll be making $50,000 a year.

As I take it all in, I feel both excited at the prospect of solvency and sick to my stomach at the prospect of working ten hours a day in a room with no windows. But beggars can't be choosers, and I'm grateful Rory came through for me.

Besides the money, the most exciting thing about the job is seeing Rory on a semi-regular basis. When my office tour is done, we spread our lunch out on the small worktable in her incredibly cluttered office.

"I know you're going to tell me you have a system, or something, but how the hell do you find anything in here?" I say, crunching on one of the tart pickles Rory discards from her sandwich.

"It's camouflage," she replies, picking up a napkin and tucking it into the collar of her dress shirt.

"Busy office, busy woman?"

"Precisely."

"You're pretty crafty."

Her lips curve into a smile. "Why, thank you."

"And thank you for the job."

"You're welcome."

"We should totally go out tonight and celebrate."

"I can't. I haven't seen Dave in a week. I need to remind him what I look like."

Dave and Rory have been together since sophomore year in college, and he's the only person I know who works harder than she does. They're scarily alike, and even resemble each other enough to sometimes be mistaken for brother and sister. On paper they make you want to puke, but in person, they're just Rory and Dave: best friends and lovers. We should all be so lucky.

"Oh, I think he'll remember you."

"Well, I'm not taking any chances."

She takes a small bite from the corner of her sandwich. The amount she eats every day wouldn't get me to eleven o'clock in the morning.

"So, I'm on my own?"

She frowns. "Should you even be going out?"

"Yes, Mom."

"It's just … sometimes you can't handle your alcohol."

"What?"

She puts down her sandwich. "Look, don't take this the wrong way, but why are you working here in the first place? Because you got drunk when you shouldn't have, right?"

Excuse me?

"It was my birthday."

"It was the day before your birthday."

"Don't wordsmith me, Rory."

"That's not really the point, is it?"

"What *is* your point?"

She hesitates.

"That maybe you should cut down. Especially if you want to succeed here."

I ball up my sandwich wrapper and stand up.

"I'll see you Monday."

"Katie, I'm only trying to help."

"Well, you're not, OK? I know I fucked up. I made a stupid mistake. But you're talking like I can't have a beer with my friends ... like I should be in ... *rehab* or something ..."

"Isn't that what that woman at *The Line* suggested?"

"She doesn't even know me."

Her mouth forms into a line.

"Right ... all she knows is that you came to an interview at nine in the morning still hammered from the night before. Silly her to think you might need some professional help."

My blood is boiling.

"Talk about the pot calling the kettle black."

"What's that supposed to mean?"

"Come on, Ror. What do you weigh now? Ninety pounds? When's the last time you ate even half a meal?"

She stares at me so intensely I think she might hit me. Then she picks up the remainder of her sandwich and shoves the entire thing into her mouth, chewing aggressively.

"That make you happy?" she says through a mouthful of food.

We stare at one another, equally furious.

I'm not sure which of us cracks first, but, suddenly, we're both laughing uncontrollably.

Rory covers her mouth with her hand to keep from spitting out bits of her sandwich.

"You know, I think that was our first fight."

"Had to happen sometime."

"Truce?"

"Truce."

Despite, and maybe because of, the fight with Rory, I arrange to meet Greer at the pub. When I get there, she's sitting at her usual stool being plied with free drinks by Steve.

Steve smirks as he hands me a beer. "Hey, birthday girl."

"What was that all about?" I ask Greer when he leaves.

"You don't remember?"

I get a flash of standing on a bar stool yelling, "Who's the birthday girl? That's me! I'm the birthday girl!"

"No ... wait ... don't tell me. I don't want to know."

"It's a good story, lass."

"Again with the stereotypical Scottish terms."

"What's wrong with being a stereotype?"

Steve brings me a shot and a beer back, waving me off when I try to pay him.

"You don't have to buy me drinks anymore, Steve. I've got a real job now."

"He's not buying you drinks. He's trying to get in my pants."

Steve colors and pretends he needs to wipe the counter further down the bar.

"You're totally taking advantage of him."

Greer tosses her hair over her shoulder and gives Steve a lascivious look. "Do you really think I could?"

"Please."

"Interesting."

I spin my stool towards Greer. "So, what's new? I feel like I haven't seen you in ages."

"It was your own self-imposed exile, remember?"

"I prefer to think of it as taking a moment. A knee if you will."

"A *knee*?"

"Yeah, you know, in football, when the coach wants to tell the team something, he says, 'Take a knee.' It means, literally, get down on one knee, but also, 'Listen up, I need your attention.'"

She frowns. "Why would you go down on one knee to listen to someone?"

"I guess it is kind of strange."

"And football players do this?"

"Yes, and I mean American football, not soccer."

"Yes, yes."

"Anyway, I was taking a time out to process the state of my life."

"And?"

"And, it turns out my life was extremely shitty."

"Was?"

I bring the shot to my nose, breathing in the sweet, hard fumes. "It's on the mend."

She raises her glass. "I'll drink to that."

"Let's."

I pour the shot down my throat and chase it with half my beer. As the alcohol spreads through my bloodstream I feel lighter than I have since my disastrous day at *The Line.*

It's good to be back.

What with one drink and another, I stumble out of bed the next day sometime after noon. I follow a trail of delicious smells to the kitchen, where Joanne is standing at the stove in her weekend uniform of roomy flannel pajamas, making a sauce

"What is that? It smells great." I pick up a spoon and try to help myself.

She swats my hand away. "It's not for people who don't answer their phones or return messages."

"What's up your butt?"

"I'm not your answering service."

"What are you talking about?"

"Some girl named Elizabeth called for you a million times yesterday."

My heart thuds to a stop. "Elizabeth from *The Line?*"

"Yeah, I think so."

"You must be joking."

But Joanne doesn't joke. She stirs the sauce vigorously a few times and puts the lid on.

"What's wrong with you? Elizabeth called. She wants you to call her back. Urgently."

I still don't completely believe her.

"What does Elizabeth sound like?"

Joanne rolls her eyes.

"She sounds like this? Like she's asking questions? All the fucking time?"

Oh. My. God! It *is* Elizabeth! She called. She wants me to call her back. Yes, yes, yes!

I'm so overcome with joy I actually hug Joanne. She stands there like a board while I jump her up and down, but I don't care. Elizabeth from *The Line* called, and all is right in the world.

I spend the rest of the day in a nervous tizzy. Even though it's Saturday, I keep checking my voicemail every fifteen minutes to see if Elizabeth's returned my call. When the sun sets and she still hasn't called, I help myself to several large glasses of Joanne's never-to-be-touched-by-her wine in a futile attempt to sleep. When that doesn't work, I flip on the E! network and watch the latest TGND coverage unfold.

TGND's been busy since I stopped watching TV all day. She broke up with Connor Parks again and went on a woe-is-me bender. Then a video of her sucking on a crack pipe surfaced. A few days ago, her parents took her to a rugged, lock-down rehab facility up north, where she has to stay for a minimum of thirty days. The footage of her entering a succession of clubs, holding a flame to a pipe, and being dropped off at rehab is played and repeated until even the anchors look bored.

I finally drift off around four in the morning, only to be awakened at eight by Joanne looking pissed and holding the phone out to me with a straight arm.

"We have to stop meeting like this," I say groggily.

"It's Elizabeth? From *The Line*?"

I grab the phone. "Hello?"

"Is that Kate?"

"Yes, this is Kate."

"This is Elizabeth from *The Line*? We met a few weeks ago?"

"Yes, hi. I remember you."

"We were wondering if you could come in for a meeting about a position that's come up? Maybe this morning at ten? I know it's

Sunday?"

"Of course I can come in for a meeting! Ten is great."

"Perfect. Come to the same place as last time?"

We say goodbye, and I spring towards the bathroom to start getting ready. The sudden movement makes my stomach turn over, but I shake it off and leap into the shower singing, for some reason, "I am, I am Superman!" over and over at the top of my lungs as I lather my hair.

Whoever said there are no second chances in life was a moron.

I arrive at *The Line*'s offices twenty minutes early with my hair brushed, my makeup done, and my clothes pressed. (I pick the suit this time, hoping some of its respectability will rub off on me.) My stomach still feels jumpy, but I chalk that up to nerves. At least I know I don't smell like alcohol, having loofahed every square inch of myself just in case.

At ten on the dot, Elizabeth appears in the Sunday-quiet lobby wearing an extremely short grey skirt and a tight blue sweater.

"Hi, Kate. How are you?"

"I'm great. Thank you so much for giving me another chance."

"Sure. So, you'll be meeting Bob? You remember him from a few weeks ago?"

I think back to the sea of faces sitting around the boardroom table. Try as I might, I can't remember Bob.

"Right, of course. Looking forward to it."

"Good. His office is two floors down?"

I take the elevator to a floor where the decor hasn't been updated in at least twenty years. It's *Miami Vice* chic, and there's something kind of seedy about the atmosphere.

Seeing no one, I push the doorbell that's recessed into the wall next to a solid wood door. A few seconds later, the door buzzes open revealing a squat, blond man who resembles Philip Seymour Hoffman, which is ironic when you think about it because PSH played a music magazine guy in *Almost Famous* and ... Focus, Katie, focus!

"Hi, Bob. Thank you so much for asking me back after ... well, you know. Anyway, I'm really excited to be here."

He gives me a tight smile. "Yes, well, when this assignment came up we thought of you ... for obvious reasons. Why don't we go to my office?"

OK, so it's an assignment, not a full-time gig, but everyone has to start somewhere, right?

I follow him along a dark hall to another nondescript brown door. He swipes a key card. The room behind the door has a long row of unoccupied fabric-divided cubicles full of abandoned coffee cups.

"Is this some kind of call center?"

"You might say that. This way."

He cuts to the right along a narrow passage through the cubicles. As I turn to follow him, I notice a paper banner hanging on the far wall. It reads, *"GOSSIP CENTRAL: IF YOU CAN'T FIND ANYTHING MEAN TO SAY, YOU CAN FIND THE DOOR."*

What the hell?

I realize Bob's striding away from me, and I hurry to catch up with him. At the end of the passage is another brown door. Bob swipes his key card once again and pushes it open.

"Sorry about all the security. But given the nature of the information we deal with, we have to take every precaution."

Since when did album reviews become top-secret information?

"Of course."

Bob points to the chair in front of his cheap-looking desk. "Have a seat."

I sit down gingerly. When is this guy going to put me out of my misery and tell me what my assignment is?

"So ... I assume Elizabeth filled you in?"

"Actually, not really."

"Well, you'll have to leave immediately because there's no telling how long she's going to be in there. Everything's all arranged, and the staff's expecting you. It'll be a minimum thirty-day assignment if all goes well, but I'm warning you, it might be longer. We'll be covering your expenses and paying the usual per-word rate. We'd like five thousand words, but we'll discuss the final length once we know what you've got."

He picks up a bulky envelope from his desk and hands it to me. "Here's the background information we've been able to put together. It's pretty extensive and will hopefully give you a place to start. Of course, you can't drink or do anything else that'll jeopardize your stay. If you get thrown out, the contract will be forfeit. Do you have any questions?"

What the fuck is this guy talking about?

"I'm sorry, but I really don't understand. What's the assignment? Where am I going?"

Bob gives me another tight smile, but this time there's an undercurrent of glee in it.

"You're going to rehab."

Made in the USA
Las Vegas, NV
18 January 2022

41739573R00083